W9-CLE-973

Poppy

Poppy

Barbara Larriva

A Ballantine/Epiphany Book
Ballantine Books • New York

A Ballantine/Epiphany Book

Library of Congress Cataloging-in-Publication Data

Larriva, Barbara, 1934–
  Poppy.

  "A Ballantine/Epiphany Book."
  I. Title.
PS3562.A7278P6   1987   813'54   87-1127
ISBN: 0-345-34308-5

Design by Holly Johnson
Manufactured in the United States of America

First Edition: October 1987
10 9 8 7 6 5 4 3 2 1

Poppy

One

Pain swept across the once-beautiful face of Allegra Alexander. The aging actress barely felt the needle the nurse pressed into her arm. She heard voices from a distance fading in and out. From some faraway place she thought she heard her doctor saying it didn't look too good. She wanted to ask him what didn't look too good, but no sound came from her lips. The swish of the drapes being closed filtered through her consciousness, and then a blessed blackness enveloped her.

Cocooned in the warm, soft blackness, Allegra became once again the beauty she had been in her prime. Tall and willowy with black hair that hugged her shoulders, the star stood apart from the crowd. Her magnificent blue eyes gazed over the thousands of fans gathered to catch a glimpse of her. She searched the multitude, but she couldn't remember who—or what—she was seeking.

"You're looking marvelous, love," crooned Ramon Novarro. Allegra flashed a brilliant smile at the handsome movie idol and then turned into the arms of her agent, Rick Elliot, who laughed and wrapped her in a bear hug.

"Come on, let's eat," he said, his hand at her waist. "You're getting skinny."

She smiled up at him. "Just fashionably thin."

On the way to the buffet table, scores of fans clustered around begging for Allegra's autograph, and she stopped to sign her name over and over in flowing script. But her eyes restlessly sought something—or someone—she couldn't find. Despite the crowded room, an aching emptiness settled on her.

"Wait here and I'll fix you a plate," Rick said and handed Allegra the silverware snugly wrapped in a white linen napkin.

She absently toyed with the rolled hem as her gaze moved across the enormous room. Suddenly her eyes were drawn to the edge of the crowd. Standing alone, back from the others, was her son Adam. Allegra's heart expanded with the joy of seeing him, but when he turned to her, the contempt on his face shriveled her soul. Her eyes pleaded for forgiveness, but Adam's face was granite—unloving, unrelenting.

Allegra cringed, backing away from the fans

4

who worshipped her. What did it matter if these thousands loved her when her own child despised her? She backed farther and farther away from the crowd, and then she felt herself falling . . . falling into nothingness. Out of a cocoon into an abyss.

"Allegra. Allegra, wake up." Small hands gently shook the withdrawn body, but the old woman fought to block out the command. She lay motionless on the hospital bed, and the little girl's hands became more insistent. "Please, Allegra. Come back," the child said, her voice breaking into Allegra's consciousness.

"I . . . don't . . . want . . . to . . . come . . . back," Allegra moaned, twisting her head from side to side.

The child gently sponged the age-wrinkled face while whispering words of encouragement. Tenderly she smoothed back a wisp of white hair that had come loose.

Forcing her eyes open, Allegra blinked several times to bring the vague form into focus. As her vision cleared, she looked into the soft gray eyes of the child leaning toward her. She clutched the sleeve of the little girl's blue cotton dress and tears spilled from the old woman's eyes. How much longer could she take the punishment of being alive? "No one cares what happens to me, child," she cried, her voice tired and weak.

"I do. God does," the girl answered matter-of-factly. Allegra impatiently dismissed the words with a feeble wave.

But a deep-rooted anger strengthened the old woman's next words. "Don't talk God to me. He was never there when I needed Him." Allegra turned on her side and stared at the little girl for several seconds. "Who are you? And what are you doing in my room?" she asked brusquely.

As the child stepped back from the bed, a splash of sunlight streamed through the window and rested softly on her small shoulder. "My name's Poppy and I came to visit you."

"Oh, no! Spare me these do-good youth groups who go around visiting the elderly and adopting grandmothers!" Allegra fumbled for her glasses and perched them on the tip of her nose. "Well, they sure named you right with that mop of red hair." She studied the girl. "So you're visiting old people, huh?"

"Well, actually, I've seen all your movies and I wanted to meet you," Poppy said, moving closer to the bed as the old woman continued to study her.

"You're way too young to have seen *my* movies,

child. How old are you anyway?" Allegra pushed herself up to a sitting position.

"I'm nine. But I've seen all of them on TV." The little voice was warm and clear and reminded the actress of a summer day after the rain. Poppy pushed a silken strand of copper hair behind her ear.

Leaning back against the unadorned pillows, the old woman had a faraway look in her eyes as she remembered moments from long ago. "They don't make movies like they used to. In the old days, way back in the thirties, they made *movie*-movies. Not like what they make today. And there was always dancing and singing and—and happiness. Lots of happiness. Even if an actor were in misery, the audience never knew it." I'm living proof of that, she added silently.

Allegra's gaze turned to Poppy again. Nodding, she said wistfully, "We always found the pot of gold at the end of the rainbow. At least, we did in the movies . . ." Her voice trailed off as she looked up at the window behind Poppy and frowned. "And who gave you permission to open the drapes?"

"Nobody. I did it on my own. You were too far into the darkness."

"This is my room, and if I want it dark in here, it'll stay dark," she snapped irritably. Suddenly Poppy's words registered and Allegra, to gather

7

time, adjusted her nightgown. She watched the little girl silently for a few moments and then said, "You mean . . . you brought me back from this—this—darkness?"

"Oh, no," Poppy assured her. "You did that yourself. Just like flowers that are drawn to sunlight and bend in prayer."

"Don't start that again, child. I haven't prayed in a hundred years and I've forgotten how." Allegra put up a hand so as not to be interrupted. "And I don't want to know how. So don't go preaching to me."

"God can wait. He's not going anywhere. When you're ready, you'll pray." Allegra flinched at the little girl's words.

"I don't like this kind of talk. If you want to visit *this* old lady you're going to have to change the subject."

Poppy merely smiled. "I heard the nurses talking in the hall. They said the doctor was going to stop by to see you this afternoon. So I'll come back after visiting hours. Okay?"

"Who cares about visiting hours? Nobody comes to visit me. Now that I'm old and sick, nobody even remembers I exist. Where are all my fans? Where are all the autograph seekers? Where are all the men who wanted me?" Allegra's voice cracked.

"What about your son?" Poppy asked quietly, and a knife slashed Allegra's heart.

"Please don't ever mention him again, child. I haven't seen him in thirty years . . ." Thirty long, miserable, empty years, she added to herself as a flicker of pain touched her eyes.

The little girl stood close to Allegra. "I'm sorry," she whispered, leaning over and kissing her, a wisp of red hair grazing the wrinkled cheek.

In an effort to veil the unexpected warmth surging through her from the child's kiss, the old woman spoke gruffly as Poppy turned to leave. "Get your hair out of your eyes."

The little girl smiled and nodded. As the door closed softly, Allegra muttered, "And leave the drapes alone next time."

Allegra leaned into her pillow and waited for Dr. Morgan. He seemed nice enough, she thought, but she hadn't known him very long—eight days, to be exact. She'd had pains in her abdomen for a couple of weeks and kept blaming them on food. When they didn't go away, but worsened instead, she made an appointment with her doctor. After examining her, he suggested she see a specialist and recommended Dr. Morgan. That same day, Dr. Morgan put her in the hospital for tests. She'd barely had time to pack a few necessities, Allegra remembered, annoyed. And after all that rushing around, they had her lying there for days on end while they poked and probed and did one test after another.

Today she was supposed to get the results. "Well," she said aloud, "if the outcome of these tests is anything like the way my life has turned out, it will be bad news indeed!"

She reached over and picked up a hand mirror lying on the table and looked at her reflection. Deep lines creased the seventy-one-year-old face. What did she expect after thirty-five years of blistering floodlights and heavy grease makeup? She frowned at the single snow-white braid that hung over her shoulder. Whatever happened to her thick shiny black hair? she wondered. But the color of her eyes hadn't dimmed over the years. Their brilliant blue gazed back at her now. Allegra shook her head. Somehow she'd never thought she'd grow old. When she was young and beautiful, and the top MGM girl, old age seemed unreal. Like dying. Those things could happen only to others. Never to her.

And aging doesn't come on gradually, she continued to muse. One day you wake up and see the face of a stranger in the mirror. Familiar—but different. And you wonder how such a shocking change could have taken place overnight. Then you mourn the loss of your youth, and cry over your mistakes, and bargain with a God who either doesn't exist or doesn't care.

What was it Seneca said? "Nothing is more disgraceful than that an old man should have nothing to show to prove that he has lived long except his years." And that goes double for women, Allegra thought bitterly.

Dr. Morgan entered the room and Allegra studied the young man before returning the mirror to the table.

He pulled the chair over to the bed and took the old woman's hand in his. "How are you feeling today, Allegra?" His face was drawn and tired despite his smile.

"Look, doctor, I know you're a busy man, so we can do without the pleasantries. You're here to give me the results of the tests, so let's get on with it." She removed her hand from his and smoothed back a few strands of loose hair.

Dr. Morgan twisted the end of his blond moustache. "We found a tumor," he said bluntly.

Allegra's face blanched and her voice trembled slightly. "And?"

"The biopsy revealed that it's malignant. I want

11

to start you right away on chemotherapy and radiation."

"No." Her voice was emphatic.

He frowned. "What do you mean—no?"

"I mean just what I said. No! No chemo and no radiation. I just want to be left alone. Now, doctor," Allegra asked as nonchalantly as if they were discussing the weather, "how much time do I have?"

Dr. Morgan shook his head sadly. "Six months to a year. Maybe a little longer if you take care of yourself . . ."

Allegra considered his words. Too long, she thought. Now that she knew the inevitable, six months seemed much too long to wait. She clenched her fists into tight balls and stared at the pink-and-white striped wallpaper. She'd lived through the golden age of talkies, she'd survived the frightening era when the studios broke apart, and she'd muddled her way through endless years of heartache and loneliness. Why couldn't she just die and get it over with?

"Allegra," he said quietly, "I'd like you to think about what I said. About chemotherapy and radiation. They could add years to your life."

She looked at him. I don't want to add years to my life, she rebutted silently.

"Well, think about it," he said and patted her hand before rising. He started for the door, then paused and asked, "Will you be okay by yourself?"

"Of course I will," she bristled. "This isn't the first crisis I've handled alone. Besides, doctor, do I have a choice?"

Dr. Morgan raised his thick, blond eyebrows and sighed. "No, I guess you don't. But at least I can make you a little more comfortable. I'll leave an order for pain pills." He hesitated at the door, staring at her as though she might change her mind. Then he walked briskly out of the room.

Allegra knew Tillie, her roommate, would be back shortly and the last thing she wanted was to listen to that magpie. The woman was an insufferable chatterbox. Ninety if she was a day, Tillie talked constantly. Allegra tried to keep her curtain closed whenever Tillie was in the room. Thank goodness she was out for therapy a good portion of the day. It was no wonder she rarely had visitors. Her constant yapping probably drove them crazy.

Turning her back to the other bed, Allegra blocked out her surroundings and looking deep inside herself, found the beautiful, adored movie star she had been long ago.

"Miss Alexander. How does it feel to be Barbara LaMarr's successor as the most beautiful woman in the world?" the reporter asked. He thrust a microphone at her as she moved toward the entrance of the exquisitely ornate Pantages Theatre.

Before she could answer, scores of reporters moved toward her until she was surrounded by men pushing and shoving and pelting her with questions.

"Please, I need room," she said breathlessly, looking around in panic for her husband.

While straining to find him in the crowd behind her, Allegra's skin began to prickle. A shudder rippled down her spine as she felt hands grabbing her. She turned around in horror to see several wild-eyed fans with outstretched arms trying to touch her. They must have broken through the police barriers set up for the movie premiere, she thought, biting down on her bottom lip to keep it from trembling. Her long, crimson fingernails dug into the palms of her hands, leaving half-moon indentations.

Suddenly, an overzealous fan yanked Allegra's ermine wrap from her shoulders and thrust a crumpled piece of paper in front of her, begging for her autograph. Dazed by fear, Allegra tried to cover her exposed arms, to shield herself from the near-hysterical mob.

Afraid her legs would no longer support her, she looked for a place to sit down. She realized the folly of such a thought as she was shuffled from side to side by the crowd. In shocked disbelief she watched the fans continue to battle the police. Then out of the corner of her eye Allegra saw her husband rushing toward her, and a flood of relief surged through her that gave her the strength she needed to get through the rest of the evening.

"Move back and let us through," he commanded as he put a protective arm around Allegra's shoulders and led her into the theatre. She smiled up at him gratefully, her tense body relaxing under the gentle pressure of his hand.

It had been like that from the day they'd met. He had been her protector, her mentor. He made all the decisions and took care of her. He selected her wardrobe from the sketches of the famous Hollywood designer, Adrian, as carefully as he selected her movie roles from the extensive MGM script library. Loved, pampered and adored not only by her fans, but by her husband—the man she loved more than life itself—Allegra knew she had everything.

She was brought back to reality by the sound of the door opening. But she remained motionless, staring up at the ceiling, trying desperately to hold onto the thread of happiness.

"Would you like me to read to you?" Poppy asked, sitting down on the edge of Allegra's bed.

Allegra continued to stare at the imaginary point in space. A single tear trickled down her wrinkled cheek, the pain of coming back to the present almost too much for her to bear.

"Maybe you'd like to play cards. I can go get some," the little girl said softly.

Allegra shook her head.

"Do you want to talk about what the doctor told you?"

Her gaze still transfixed, Allegra spoke in a tired, defeated voice, ignoring the child's questions. "Why aren't you with the other children? Why are you hanging around here? The last thing I need is a red-headed guardian angel hovering over me."

Poppy took one of Allegra's blue-veined hands in hers.

Suddenly dropping her gaze and blinking, the actress jerked her hand away. "Go back where you belong. You're too young to be spending all your time with an old lady."

"Oh, phooey. You're not old. You're Allegra Alexander, remember? The beautiful movie star. The queen of tinsel town. I read that in an old movie magazine. I think it was *Photoplay*. No, maybe it was *Modern Screen*. Well, anyway, you were on the cover." Poppy blew at the strand of hair that perpetually fell over her brow.

Allegra's bittersweet laughter filled the small room. "You're impossible, child. Queen of tinsel

16

town indeed! I look more like the crumpled tinsel scattered all over the floor the day after Christmas. But you do make me laugh. Goodness knows I haven't done that in a dog's age."

"You talk funny, Allegra."

"Yeah, well so do you. Now go back where you belong. I want to rest."

Before Allegra could protest, Poppy threw her arms around the actress and held her close. "I think I'll adopt you as my grandmother, but let's keep it our secret, okay?"

The old woman stiffened and vigorously resisted the sudden desire to hold this beautiful child in her arms—arms that had been empty for too many years. After swallowing the lump in her throat, she said hoarsely, "Enough," and watched the copper-haired child slip out the door.

A few minutes later Tillie was brought back to the room, but Allegra ignored her and stared at the late afternoon shadows on the wall. She lay motionless, shaken by a yearning so intense it frightened her—a yearning to love again.

Two

Allegra didn't sleep much anymore. What could
have been the perfect escape had been taken
away—like everything else that mattered to her.

So it didn't surprise her when she awakened at
three in the morning. Not wanting to wake Tillie
with a light, she lay quietly in the darkened room
thinking about Poppy and all the questions the little
girl was forcing her to face.

She thought about prayer—remembering the
last time she'd prayed and her vow never to pray
again. She thought about God—the God who had
ignored her in her deepest hour of need. She thought
about her life—the terrible mistakes she'd made that
caused her to feel despicable, worthless, but most of
all unlovable.

Poppy had said that God loved her. But how
could He? If she, Allegra Alexander, couldn't stand
herself—how could God? And why should He? She

had stopped loving, shut down her feelings, and closed herself off from everything—including God—thirty-eight years ago. Surely He wouldn't be waiting around for her to make a reversal. What a joke. No, God had never loved her. Not then, not now.

Especially not during those long, empty years when she'd had to learn to live without Jim and Adam. Allegra had continued acting and stayed at the top of her profession until she was almost fifty-five. But then fewer and fewer good scripts were offered her. Like Garbo, rather than take supporting roles or work in B movies, she left the screen without officially retiring.

At first she travelled almost constantly, but when the novelty wore off she settled down and bought a house.

Allegra furnished the large, two-story house with a combination of faded antiques, garage sale specials, and a few of her treasured possessions that she'd kept in storage after she'd sold the house she and Jim had lived in from the day they were married.

As she arranged the furniture haphazardly, she tried to block thoughts of Jim from her mind. Of course it had been useless. Each time she picked up one of the lovely pieces he had chosen years ago for their home, she found herself fondling it. It made no difference whether it was the exquisite tapestry woven with gold threads or the heirloom clock, its dark wood rich and warm. When her fingers touched the memories, Jim came alive again.

While caressing the soft white velvet love seat, Allegra remembered how he used to tease her about her ineptitude when it came to decorating. How many times had he told her it was a good thing she'd decided on acting rather than interior design? His gentle gibes had always made her laugh. But in that cold, lonely house, Allegra realized she hadn't laughed for a long, long time.

Her friends and family were all gone, and her older sister, Stella, who'd never forgiven Allegra for the way she'd treated Adam, was gone as well.

As Allegra looked around the jumbled room of mismatched pieces, she had to fight back the bitter taste in her mouth at Jim's senseless death—and her senseless life.

Allegra shook her head to try to stop the past from suffocating her. She closed her eyes, as if closing them would shut out the painful thought that she was incapable of being loved. But the thought stayed with her, tormenting her.

She wished for death, for only in death would she be free of the pain of living. Sleep came instead. And dreams. The dreams wove into memories of

exquisite lost days when she was young and happy
and in love.

The day she met Jim Walsh, he had stood there
in his bathroom, staring in disbelief at her in his tub.
"Tell me, young lady, are you a misplaced mermaid?" asked the famous producer.

Twenty-year-old Alexis Riggs looked up into
eyes as blue as her own and watched the corners
crinkle into deep laugh lines. Her heart sank.

As far back as Alexis could remember, all she'd
ever wanted was to be a movie star. She began hanging out in Hollywood soda fountains when she was
seventeen, hoping to be noticed by a major movie
mogul. When that failed, she knew she'd have to
take bolder action. She convinced a friend who
worked at the Beverly Wilshire Hotel to borrow the
key to Jim Walsh's suite. Her plan was to sneak in
when he was gone, fill his tub with bubble bath, and
wait to be discovered.

Somehow it hadn't worked out the way she'd
expected. He seemed amused rather than impressed.

"Mermaid? No . . . I . . . you see . . ." Her face
flushed with embarrassment and she wished she
were indeed seaworthy so she could slither quietly
down the drain and get away from those piercing
blue eyes. Alexis shivered and sat up straighter so

he would be sure to see that she was wearing a bathing suit.

"Here," he said, smiling as he handed her a fluffy white towel. "My study is straight down the hall to the right. I'll wait for you there." At the door he turned around to look at her and said, "You do have some clothes with you, don't you?" His eyes glittered with amusement.

She nodded, feeling a rush of color darken her cheeks again.

He started down the hall. "By the way, what's your name?" he called in a voice Alexis quickly classified as sexy.

"Alexis. Alexis Riggs." She waited a few minutes. When she was sure he had gone, she stepped out of the tub, took off the bathing suit, squeezed the water out of it and stuffed it into the bottom of her purse. After she rubbed herself vigorously with the soft towel, she let it drop to the floor. "What'll I do now?" she moaned. "He's absolutely gorgeous! Tall, blond, and those incredible blue eyes . . ." She'd expected him to be old and fat. Well, he was *kind* of old—probably forty. But he was so handsome. This certainly wasn't working out the way she'd envisioned it, she thought as she ran a comb through her damp, tangled hair. And now he wanted to talk to her. Oh, dear, what could she say to him that wouldn't sound young and stupid—like she felt?

Maybe he was going to file charges for trespassing? Well, there was only one way to find out. Quickly slipping into her dress, the only good one she owned, Alexis squared her shoulders, picked up her portfolio, and marched down the brown-carpeted hall to meet her fate.

With a shy hesitancy, she pushed open the study door and stood quietly watching the late afternoon sun bounce off the producer's burnished gold sideburns as he stared down at the papers on his desk. When he looked up, Alexis felt her legs weaken. She wanted to blame the rubbery sensation in her limbs on their being waterlogged, but her thumping heart told her differently. To make matters worse, she couldn't pull her eyes from his.

Without taking his gaze from hers, he stood up and walked around the desk. Capturing her hand in a strong grip, he led Alexis to the brown leather sofa, pushed aside the beige velour throw pillows and sat down next to her.

"Okay, young lady, tell me what this is all about." He was still holding her hand and Alexis felt light-headed.

"Well, you see, Mr. Walsh . . ."

"Jim," he corrected.

24

"Well, you see . . . Jim . . . I have a friend who works here at this hotel—we'll just skip her name . . ."

"Of course," he smiled, squeezing her hand.

Alexis breathlessly told him how she found her way into his bathtub, feeling more foolish with each word.

"We thought you'd gone out to lunch," she finished lamely.

"I was at the studio discussing a contract," he said, his eyes bright with mirth.

"I kind of figured something like that had happened," she said softly.

"And all your bubbles burst."

Alexis nodded. "And the water got cold." They joined in laughter.

"Are you warm enough now?" he asked as he rubbed her hands.

"Oh, yes," she said, sounding a little more eager than she meant to.

"Good. Now let me take a look at your pictures."

An hour later Jim closed the portfolio and transferred his attention back to Alexis sitting quietly next to him. He searched her face as if trying to extract something from her features and suddenly Jim laughed vivaciously.

"That's it! Allegra! Allegra Alexander."

"Who's Allegra Alexander?"

"You. No more Alexis Riggs." Jim rose and went to the small refrigerator behind the bar. He popped open a bottle of champagne and poured two glasses.

Handing one to Alexis, he raised his glass in a toast. "I hereby christen you Allegra Alexander."

She stared up at him. Did that mean he liked her pictures? Oh, God, she hoped so. She raised her glass to Jim's and held her breath, waiting.

"How would you like to star in my next movie?" he asked in a serious voice and Alexis stared, dumbfounded.

"Well?" he prompted, grinning.

Unable to speak, she jumped up and threw her arms around his neck, nearly knocking him off balance. Her crazy, wonderful dream had come true. She was going to be a movie star! A real, live movie star. "Alexis Riggs is gone forever. I am now Allegra Alexander," she chanted.

Unmindful of the champagne that spilled onto the plush white carpet, Jim wrapped her in his arms, repeating her name again and again. "Allegra Alexander, you're the most beautiful thing that ever happened to me. And tomorrow I'm going to introduce you to the big boss at MGM—Louis B. Mayer."

Her eyes widened in disbelief. "Louis B. Mayer?"

Jim nodded. "I'll call and make the arrangements."

The next day, as they drove to Culver City, Allegra toyed nervously with the ruffles on the lavender dress Jim had insisted on buying for her when he learned the dress she'd worn the previous day was her Sunday best.

Jim patted her hand. "Don't worry about a thing, honey. He's going to absolutely love you."

Allegra smiled weakly in answer.

They pulled up to the MGM gate and were waved on as the security guard recognized Jim.

Jim pulled into his assigned parking space and turned off the engine. He took Allegra's hand and, grinning wickedly, said, "Let me tell you a little about Mayer's office before we go in. It'll keep you from staring."

Allegra doubted that. She'd read too much about the ostentatious Louis B. Mayer.

"His office is carved from two floors of MGM's executive building, and it's a gilded tower that reflects a soft light down onto his desk. He had the top weavers in France make him a path that leads to his desk, a rug of silver threads with a white fur runner." He stopped and smiled at Allegra before

27

continuing. "Oh, yes, and a thick carpet conceals a platform that provides Mayer with a little more height than nature gave him."

"It sounds so theatrical—so pompous."

"It is. Ready?"

"Ready." She smiled, feeling a little better now that she knew the great Mr. Mayer wasn't actually going to tower over her.

Mayer's office was everything Jim had said and more. And although he was short, Louis B. Mayer was still most intimidating.

"So you're the young beauty my friend here raved about on the phone yesterday. Let me have a good look at you."

Allegra glanced at Jim, who nodded his encouragement. Standing up slowly, she walked toward the famous movie mogul, the highest paid man in America.

"Not bad, not bad," Mayer murmured appreciatively.

Jim leaned back in the overstuffed beige leather chair and steepled his fingers under his chin. "What do you think, Louie, about Allegra playing the lead in *A Winter's Song*? You said you wanted an unknown female with star quality."

Mayer nodded and closed his eyes. "Who's signed for the male lead?"

"Clark Gable."

Allegra spun around. "Clark Gable?" she gasped.

"Let's discuss it over lunch." Mayer stood up and walked around the desk to Allegra. "I'd take you to the Brown Derby so you could try their grapefruit cake, but I have a busy afternoon planned. We'll eat here. Besides, it's good for you to be seen at the studio commissary. Wait and see what happens. In an hour everyone's going to be buzzing about you, wondering who you are. Watch out for jealous fangs, by the way."

For some peculiar reason, all Allegra's whirling young mind could focus on as they stepped into the elevator was: what in the world is grapefruit cake?

Mayer led Allegra and Jim to his private table, where they could see the rest of the commissary and also be seen. Without asking their preferences, he ordered three lobster salads, a loaf of warm bread with sweet butter, and coffee.

Jim, having known and worked with Mayer for years, seemed to take everything in stride. But Allegra was mesmerized by Mayer's authoritative manner. As delicious as the food was, she was too busy taking in everything to appreciate it.

Studying the large room, she nudged Jim. "Look," she whispered breathlessly, nodding to their right. "Isn't that Jean Harlow and Norma Shearer?"

Her naive awe brought a protective look to Jim's face. Touching her cheek, he said it was indeed Harlow and Shearer.

Allegra's face beamed with pleasure. A few minutes later, she stared at a corner table half-hidden from view by potted shrubbery. Jim followed her gaze to the beautiful woman in a rough tweed coat and a slouch hat, sitting alone.

Allegra couldn't believe it! She was in the same room as the exciting, mysterious Greta Garbo. She squeezed Jim's hand. "I'll never forget this day as long as I live."

Mayer glanced at his gold watch. "I'll be leaving you two now." Looking directly at Allegra, he said, "In this business you either have it or you don't. I think you've got it." To Jim, he said, "Test her for *A Winter's Song*."

"Test?" Jim echoed.

"Just a formality. She's got the part." Mayer turned and walked from the room.

Jim took Allegra's hand and raised it to his lips. "We did it."

Allegra's radiant smile transformed her. "*We* didn't do it," she replied softly. "*You* did."

From that day on they were inseparable. Allegra

had never believed in love at first sight—she thought that happened only in the movies. But Jim changed her mind about so many things.

Allegra wondered many times if perhaps her initial feelings for Jim stemmed from her being fatherless from the age of three. Since her mother had never remarried, Allegra supposed Jim represented some sort of father figure to her.

In their early days together, Jim made it clear he would always be there for her—that she could always count on his help, his support. So she couldn't help but wonder whether it was a mutual feeling—that she was a daughter figure to him. Even his teasing was like a father teasing his daughter.

Whatever its beginnings, their relationship quickly turned to a mature, exciting love. Although he was twenty years her senior, they were married six months later.

As Allegra blossomed in the warmth of her marriage with Jim, she skyrocketed to fame as Hollywood's brightest new star. But she never allowed her public life to interfere with her marriage. Jim was always number one, the center of her world. Just as movie magnate Irving Thalberg took care of his wife Norma Shearer, Jim took care of Allegra.

Adam James Walsh arrived one week before Allegra's twenty-third birthday. He was strong and healthy, the image of his father. No other parents had ever been more adoring and happy than Allegra and Jim were with this remarkable child they had created out of their love for each other.

"I brought my two favorite people some presents," Jim announced, his arms laden with gifts as he entered the maternity ward.

Allegra laughed as he struggled to kick the door closed while balancing an armful of elegantly wrapped boxes, each one tied with a blue ribbon. "Where are we going to put them all?" she asked, sweeping her arm toward the pile of presents.

"I'll take everything home to the nursery tonight. But first I want to see how you like these."

Allegra unwrapped a baseball mitt, a bat, a train set, a cowboy hat, and several books. "Oh, Jim, just what he needs," she teased. "He'll be kept busy for years. But you're wonderful!" she added lovingly, her voice lowering.

"And this is for you," Jim said softly as he handed her a small box, his hand lingering on hers.

"Oh, darling, I don't need anything. I have everything I could possibly want—you . . . Adam . . . my career."

"It's a token of my thankfulness for the miraculous gift you've given me." Allegra tore off the wrapping paper. Her fingers found the spring and

32

the box clicked open. She gasped at the elegant emerald ring lying on soft black velvet.

"It's your birthstone."

"I know. I know. Thank you, darling," she cried as he slipped the exquisite ring on her finger. While tears of happiness blurred her vision and ran down her face, Allegra hugged and kissed the man she loved more than anything in the world. Jim— her first lover, her husband, and now the father of her child.

But then one rainy night, everything was taken away from her . . .

Suddenly her warm, sweet dream of Jim and their baby turned into a nightmare. She imagined the ear-splitting crash of the car, and began screaming. Her aging body thrashed in the hospital bed as she struggled to wake herself.

She awoke, wondering whether she had screamed aloud. Her nightgown was wet and stuck to her body and she pushed back the damp hair that had fallen across her face. Unable to control her trembling, she lay there shaking. She glanced over at Tillie, who was snoring softly.

Why did she keep having this torturous nightmare? Why couldn't she forget?

Poppy's whisper cut through Allegra's torment. "Allegra, I couldn't sleep. Would you like some company?" The little girl stood in the doorway, her tousled red hair illuminated by the light from the hall.

The old woman's eyes were glazed as she turned toward the tiny voice.

"What's the matter?" Poppy hurriedly closed the door behind her, switched on the small bedside lamp, then pulled the curtain.

Allegra stared at her blankly, blinking, as if seeing her for the first time. "I . . . I had a terrible nightmare, but I'm all right now." She shuddered, hugging herself.

"Your nightgown's soaking wet. Let me help you change. Where do they keep extra ones?" she whispered.

Without waiting for an answer, Poppy opened a drawer and began rummaging through it. "Here's one," she said, lifting out a drab, shapeless hospital gown. "Not very pretty, but at least it's dry." She helped Allegra sit up and remove her wet gown.

Emotionally drained from the nightmare, the old woman was too weak to protest Poppy's ministrations. Even now she could hear the sound of the crashing car—impossible, for at the time of the accident she had been miles away. She knew from years of experience that there was nothing to do but wait for the terrible sound to go away.

Perhaps if she talked to this red-headed miniature Florence Nightingale the dream would fade sooner this time.

"Don't worry," Allegra said when she saw Poppy glance in the direction of Tillie's bed. "She's as deaf as a doughnut. Takes her hearing aid out at night, too. Nothing less than an explosion under her pillow would wake her. Don't be so rough, child, I'm an old lady."

Poppy looked up, smiling because Allegra sounded like herself again.

"I'm sorry. I was just trying to hurry up and get you comfortable. It can't be much fun wearing a wet nightgown."

Allegra's eyes softened and Poppy watched the change. "Do you want to talk about your nightmare?"

"So you can get scared?" Allegra asked gruffly.

"But *I'll* know it's not real."

Allegra looked at the child through tortured blue eyes. "It's not that kind of nightmare. It's personal—something I've learned to live with for thirty-eight years."

"Sometimes talking about things like that make them less . . ."

"No, child, this is my cross. It can't be shared."

"Well then, would you like me to sing for you?" Poppy asked eagerly.

"Sing?" Allegra echoed.

"It'll only take me a couple of minutes to get my guitar. I know lots of songs."

"You'll wake up the whole hospital! Except for Tillie, that is. That magpie wears herself out with her constant chatter. It's no wonder she can sleep through anything."

Poppy laughed. "I don't sing loud." She was already headed for the door. "Don't go away," she called softly over her shoulder. "I'll be right back."

"Ha, where would I go even if I could get out of this place?" Allegra mumbled. As she leaned back against the pillows, a mistiness blurred her vision. Hadn't Adam been about Poppy's age when he learned to play the guitar? He hadn't been very good at singing though, she smiled, remembering. She hoped this flower child would be better.

With the strap of her guitar slung around her neck, Poppy quietly opened the door and tiptoed in. She moved noiselessly to the bed.

"I'm back," she announced.

"I can see that. Well, first get the hair out of your eyes and then let's get on with the concert so I can get some sleep."

"Okay." She brushed her hair behind her ears. "Is there anything special you'd like to hear?"

"No. Just something quiet that doesn't bring the nurses running in."

"Don't worry, I won't be loud."

Poppy perched on the edge of the chair, and placed the guitar on her knees. As she ran her fingers over the strings, tuning the instrument, Allegra closed her eyes.

When a poignant melody began, Allegra opened her eyes and studied the copper head bent over the guitar. She watched Poppy's small fingers caress the taut strings. The little girl's soft, melodious voice floated across the room.

Please don't be afraid, my friend
I am by your side
Let me take your hand in mine
Lift it, swing it wide.
Come with me, my new found friend
Let me lead the way
To a simple, quiet place
Where your heart can pray.
Please don't be afraid, my friend . . .

Poppy finished singing and looked up to find Allegra watching her.

"That was lovely, child. I don't think I've ever heard that piece before. Is it new?"

"I just made it up," Poppy said as she lifted the strap from around her neck.

"You just *made it up*? Just like that?" Allegra was impressed.

Poppy shrugged her small shoulders. "I like to make up songs. I do it all the time."

"Well, it was nice of you to sing this one for me. Who taught you how to play the guitar?"

"My father."

"And did he teach you to sing and make up songs?"

"No. I did that on my own." The little girl smiled winsomely.

Allegra sighed, feeling suddenly relaxed. "Well, I think I'll be able to get back to sleep now."

"Do you want me to stay with you a while?" Poppy placed her guitar gently against the wall.

Allegra shook her head. "Just leave the night-light on for me," she answered softly, turning on her side.

Poppy plumped up her pillow and tucked the sheet gently around the old woman. "Good night," she whispered and kissed Allegra's cheek.

"Out!" Allegra grumbled, trying to hide the tenderness this child had awakened in her.

Poppy

Poppy picked up her guitar and, as she walked to the door, resumed her song in her quiet, sweet voice. *Please don't be afraid, my friend.*

Allegra softened. "Good night, child." She watched Poppy carry the guitar that was almost as big as she was.

Stopping at the door, Poppy smiled and blew Allegra a kiss. Then she gently closed the door behind her.

Allegra almost returned the kiss, but caught herself in time. Involuntarily she thought of Adam. Sweet, cuddly Adam who had bounced with glee when she blew him kisses and told him they landed on his nose. Touching his little face with pudgy fingers he'd scamper off to the mirror in search of the kisses. Suddenly he'd realize it was a game and would come running back and blow a kiss to Allegra—as Poppy had just done.

Safer to think of Poppy, Allegra told herself, pursing her lips and tapping them. Then she nodded pensively. Who was this child who was inching her way into her heart, who wandered into her room at the times Allegra needed someone the most? Allegra promised herself she'd find out.

Three

The next day Allegra found herself in an unwanted conversation with Tillie, and Poppy was forgotten for the moment.

"Look," Allegra said heatedly to Tillie, "this isn't a country club. I'd rather not have to listen to your constant chitchat."

With her thin, mousy hair in rollers, Tillie sat on the edge of the bed, her short, skinny legs dangling over the side. "You know what, Allegra Alexander? You might have been a famous movie star once, but you're nothing but a nasty old lady now."

"You're calling *me* old?"

"You put the emphasis on the wrong word, dearie. I'm calling you *nasty*! And while I'm at it, you're also ill-tempered. And inconsiderate. No wonder you never have any visitors."

Allegra blanched and thought of Adam—the one visitor she'd give anything to see.

Tillie covered her mouth as if to take back the harsh words. "I'm sorry. I don't know what got into me. I can't imagine what ever made me say such terrible things to you . . ."

Tillie was interrupted by Betty, the sprightly, petite nurse whose blonde curls bounced with her every step. "Time for therapy, dear. We're going to have you up and out of this hospital real soon," she said, taking Tillie's arm.

Not soon enough, Allegra said to herself.

"By the way, Allegra, it's such a lovely spring day today, we're letting some of our patients spend a little time outdoors. Would you like to sit outside for a while this afternoon?"

"Not if I have to go out there in this starched sheet!" Allegra answered, pointing to the hospital nightgown Poppy had helped her into the night before.

The nurse suppressed a smile. "If you have a nightgown with you I'll arrange to have Jean help you change and take you out this afternoon. Her shift starts at three."

"Of course I have a nightgown with me. It's in the drawer," Allegra snapped impatiently. Then in a quieter voice she added, "But it needs to be laundered."

Betty, unperturbed by the old woman's mood

swings, answered calmly, "I'll see what I can do for you." Her eyes rested softly on the actress. "Jean will come by after three. In the meantime, if you need anything just ring the buzzer." She and Tillie left the room and Allegra was alone.

Her spirits drooped. She hated being alone worse than she hated having Tillie in the next bed. Actually, she didn't mind having the woman there. It was her incessant gabbing that grated on Allegra's nerves.

Poppy was the only one who seemed to understand how she felt. Allegra wondered if she'd see the little redhead again. Well, it really doesn't matter, she thought. I've been a loner for so long now that any kind of relationship is an intrusion. It will probably be just as well if Poppy doesn't come around anymore.

After lunch Allegra dozed off into a dreamless sleep. She woke up when a nurse came clattering into the room.

"Ready?" The heavy-set, dark-haired young woman stood by the bed.

"Where's Betty?" Allegra asked groggily, peering at the name tag pinned over the nurse's large bosom.

"She's gone off duty now. She left instructions for me to take you outdoors. I'm Jean."

"Of course. I remember now."

"Do you want me to help you change?" Jean had Allegra's freshly laundered nightgown folded over her arm.

"I'm not an invalid yet. I can do it myself," Allegra retorted sharply.

"Now don't get excited. It's not good for you."

Why am I taking my frustrations out on this poor girl? Allegra asked herself. She's just doing her job. In a calmer voice she said, "Who laundered my gown?"

Jean looked embarrassed. "I had a few extra minutes. It was nothing."

Allegra watched her, waiting for her to go on.

"I've always been a fan of yours, Miss Alexander. I heard you had no family and I . . ."

She's right. Allegra Alexander has no family. No husband. No son. Nobody. The actress swallowed and turned her head to the window to hide her pain.

Whatever happened to Kate Hepburn? she asked herself. Years ago she and Kate had been extremely close, but somewhere along the way their friendship had faded. She hadn't seen Kate in more than thirty years. Just one of many losses Allegra had learned to bear.

She turned back to the nurse and asked, "Will you be staying with me outside?"

"For a little while. We'll find a place where you can sit quietly and enjoy the sunshine. Then, if you want, I can leave you there alone. Most patients like time by themselves—especially outdoors. It must have something to do with nature."

Allegra nodded and let Jean help her change into her nightgown and robe. Then Jean settled her into the wheelchair.

"I'm perfectly capable of walking, you know." A sharp pain in her abdomen cut off her words and she winced.

"I'm sure you are, but the hospital prefers its patients to use a wheelchair when they leave their floor."

Playing with the folds of the coverlet Jean had placed on her lap, Allegra tried to make her voice sound casual. "Have you noticed a little girl, about nine years old—with red hair—around today?"

"No. But children aren't allowed on this floor. Ready to go?"

Allegra nodded. She didn't question the nurse further. Thoughts of Poppy were abandoned as Jean eased the wheelchair out the door.

Poppy

. . .

It was wonderful to be outside again. It had been much too long since she'd smelled fresh grass. The sweet, warm air contrasted sharply with the sterility of the hospital, and seemed to wrap itself around Allegra, relaxing her.

When Jean wheeled her near a lilac tree, Allegra suddenly asked to stop.

"I'd like to stay here a while. And there's no need for you to stay with me. I'll be fine."

"If you're sure you'll be all right, I do have some things I need to get done."

"Just so I don't get left here after dark." Allegra's eyes sparkled and Jean laughed.

"Whenever you're ready to go back, any one of the nurses out here will gladly take you. Okay?"

Allegra looked at the white uniforms dotting the area. She nodded and Jean hurried back into the main wing of the hospital.

A touch of freedom, Allegra sighed, looking up at the blue cloudless sky. Not much, but a touch. How wonderful it was to be free of those four hospital walls, especially the striped one that seemed sometimes to close in on her.

She closed her eyes, and felt the soothing warmth of the sun penetrate her body. The heavy fragrance of purple and white lilacs filled the air and she sighed as she inhaled their heady perfume.

The familiar scent pulled Allegra back through the years. She and Jim had planted huge flowering lilac bushes in their yard. Every spring Allegra would cut the fragrant blossoms and fill every vase she owned with the delightful flowers. Lilacs were her favorite, and Jim always teased her because she preferred those simple flowers to long-stemmed roses. Tears welled at the memory. Oh, Jim, where are you now? she cried inwardly. Are you waiting for me?

Moments later she saw Poppy walking toward her. The red-haired moppet stopped in front of the wheelchair. "Would you like to go for a walk?" she asked enthusiastically.

Allegra smiled. "I imagine you mean that fig-uratively, child?"

"If that means I don't expect you to get up and walk, you're right," Poppy giggled.

"Let's go then. I'd like to see the rest of the grounds. So far, the outdoors has the indoors beat by a mile."

Poppy wheeled Allegra down a path. A few minutes later, they stopped near an old wooden bench nestled under a large oak tree, its branches spread far out over the smooth lawn.

Inching the wheelchair close to the bench, Poppy secured the brake and sat down next to Allegra.

The old woman turned to face Poppy and said abruptly, "I think it's time you told me about yourself."

"Oh, I'd much rather listen to you talk about your life in Hollywood. One of my dad's old movie magazines said you were discovered by a famous Hollywood producer in his bathtub. Is that true? What did he do when he found you?"

Allegra's eyes became young and dreamy. "He married me."

"Just like in the movies!" Poppy exclaimed.

"Better than the movies, because it was real," the old woman said, her eyes alight.

"And like a fairy tale you lived happily ever after."

"Happily, but not ever after. My beloved Jim died thirteen years after we were married." Allegra's eyes filled with tears. "Thirteen years probably sounds like a lifetime to someone as young as you, but it wasn't nearly long enough. I wanted it to go on for many more years. I wanted it—forever." Allegra looked away, her voice almost inaudible as she gazed back through the mists of time. "When Jim died, I died too. Oh, I kept walking and talking and even acting. But I was dead, child. As dead as Jim."

She bowed her head. "I want to go back to the room now." The pain in Allegra's heart was every bit as real as the pain in her body.

Poppy put her small hand on Allegra's shoulder and the old woman felt a warmth seep through her, easing her suffering.

"There's a garden on the other side of the building with pretty flowers. I go there to talk to God. It's peaceful and mostly it's quiet except for the sound of the fountain and the birds that like to play in the water. Would you like me to take you there tomorrow morning?" Poppy asked, removing her hand from Allegra's shoulder.

"Certainly not if I have to be part of a ritual," she snapped.

"Oh, Allegra, you say the funniest things. I just want you to see how beautiful it is early in the morning. You don't have to talk to God if you don't want to." Poppy touched Allegra's arm. "But what if He wants to talk to you?"

Before Allegra could form a protest, Poppy wheeled her back to the lilac tree. Then she bent down and kissed Allegra's cheek and walked away. The old woman watched her go and then looked up to see Jean coming toward her.

"Ready to go in now?" Allegra nodded and Jean began pushing the chair back to the hospital.

The next morning Allegra was awakened by the sun bursting through the window. "If that child doesn't keep her hands off those drapes, I'm going to scream," she said out loud, forgetting Tillie was in the next bed. Then she grinned to herself. "Well, she certainly keeps me going . . ." She stopped in mid-sentence. Was that what Poppy was trying to do? Keep her going? Allegra's eyes were drawn to the window. The drapes had been closed when she went to sleep the night before. Does this mysterious child wander in and out of the room at night? she asked herself. And where is she now? Allegra looked at the small clock on the table. Six o'clock.

"Is that you talking to yourself?" Tillie asked from across the room as she pulled pink foam rollers out of her hair.

Allegra let out a deep sigh of exasperation. "Yes, it's me. Who else would it be?"

"Well if you can talk to yourself, why can't you talk to me?" Tillie asked, trying to get a comb through her frizzy hair.

"All right. What do you want to talk about?"

"Well, nothing right now. I have to go to the bathroom," she said and left the room.

Allegra closed her eyes and counted to ten.

Suddenly the door squeaked open and a mop of red hair popped in. "Hi! Are you ready?"

Relief flooded Allegra at the sight of the little girl. Hiding her feelings, she snapped, "I will be as soon as you get my robe for me. You don't think I'm going out in a flimsy nightgown, do you? And, child, will you please get that hair out of your eyes?"

Poppy giggled behind small fingers before pushing her hair back. Composing herself, she said, "Allegra Alexander go out in a flimsy nightgown? No way. And I don't expect you to go out in yesterday's robe either. Wait a minute. I've got something for you out in the hall."

Poppy returned seconds later carrying a plain white sack. She crossed the room and pulled a silky lavender robe out of the bag. Holding it up, she waited expectantly for Allegra's reaction.

The old woman's mouth opened but no sound came out. She could only stare. The lilac robe was exactly like the one Jim had bought her when they were first married. But how could that be?

"Don't you like it?" Poppy asked, carrying it closer to the bed.

Startled, Allegra stammered, "Why . . . why yes. That's my favorite color, child. How in the world did you know . . . ?" Allegra's blue eyes searched the child's.

Poppy grinned. "Oh, that was easy. You wore this color in all your movies."

"Most of my movies were in black and white," Allegra said slowly.

"Then I must have seen it in a movie magazine. My dad had bunches of old movie magazines I used to look through. They always told the actresses' favorite colors and favorite foods . . ." Her voice trailed off.

Allegra looked deeply into Poppy's gray eyes and nodded. "Of course . . ."

"Do you like it?" The little girl's eyes sparkled.

"It's beautiful. But where in the world did you . . ."

"If we don't hurry," Poppy broke in, "we'll miss the best time of the morning. Here, let me help you."

Allegra's mind was full of questions but she remained unusually quiet while Poppy helped her with the robe. She knew this child wasn't a figment of her imagination. Those little hands touching her were real. But who was she? Where had she come from? Allegra sighed. She would just have to wait . . . and watch.

Poppy seemed to peruse the change in her. "Are you mad at me?"

"Of course not, child. Why in the world would I be mad at you?"

"I don't know, but you're awfully quiet," she said as she handed Allegra a light afghan and wheeled her out of the building.

"You like it better when I yell at you? Okay. The drapes were open this morning and I wasn't too happy when the sun woke me up." Allegra expected a denial.

"I wanted to be sure you'd be awake so we could get an early start."

Allegra shook her head slowly, not sure what to make of Poppy's answer.

As they approached the garden, Allegra suddenly realized they hadn't encountered anyone on the way. Not a nurse, not a patient—no one. She turned around, almost afraid the child wouldn't be there.

Poppy's small hand gently squeezed Allegra's shoulder. "It's okay, Allegra. I'm here."

A shudder rippled through the old woman's body. Does this child read my mind, too? she wondered. Shaking her head, Allegra knew she had to gain control of her overworked imagination. After all, Poppy's comment was one any nine-year-old might make if someone turned around frantically the way she had.

The old woman sighed deeply until she felt herself relax. Why was she fretting over imaginary problems and wasting such a lovely morning? God knows, there weren't many good ones.

Poppy wheeled Allegra to a wooden bench near a fountain. "Do you mind if I go into the garden for a few minutes?"

"No, of course not," Allegra answered and watched Poppy bend over a shrub of flowers, her silky hair hiding her face. A few minutes later she returned with a bouquet of white gardenias. She had fastened them together with a thin piece of rusty wire.

Poppy smiled and handed the fragrant flowers to Allegra. "These are for you."

The old woman lowered her head to the bouquet, more to hide her quivering lips than to smell the flowers. When she looked up, Poppy was sitting on the bench, her eyes closed, her small face raised to the heavens. She could almost feel the energy emanating from the little girl's body.

As she watched Poppy, Allegra's eyes grew heavy and then closed. Later, the memory of a beautiful, haunting dream in which Adam had smiled at her lovingly came rushing back. She went over every detail of the dream in her mind, staring blindly at the garden, the flowers a blur of colors.

Oh, Adam, she cried silently as she looked up at the clear azure sky. I'm so sorry for the way I treated you. But when your father died, I died too. I felt nothing. I stopped loving. Because of my self-ishness I neglected you. I turned away from you when you needed me most. Will you ever be able to find it in your heart to forgive me, son?

Allegra bowed her head and buried her face in her hands, unshed tears stinging her eyelids.

Poppy's light touch on her shoulder brought her back to her surroundings. "I think it's time to go."

Allegra nodded, clutching the gardenias close to her heart as Poppy pushed the wheelchair silently along the path.

The room was empty. When Allegra was settled in her bed once again, she lay back and studied the mysterious child with the flowing red hair as she arranged the gardenias in a glass.

"Aren't you going to ask me what happened out there?"

"I don't need to ask," Poppy said and turned to face Allegra.

"What do you mean, you don't need to ask?"

Poppy picked up Allegra's slender hand. "God talked to you."

"Nobody talked to me. I had a dream."

The little girl smiled. "Was it that nightmare you always have?"

Allegra's blue eyes softened and she murmured, "No, this was a beautiful dream about Adam . . ."

Poppy bent over to kiss the old woman's cheek and whispered softly, "That was God talking to you."

Four

Could Poppy be right? Allegra wondered. Could my beautiful dream about Adam be a sign from God? Sitting up in bed abruptly, Allegra pushed her hair back. I must be hysterical, she thought, or maybe even demented—to think God would bother giving me a sign. "God talking, to me, hrumph," she snorted. "I doubt if He talks to saints any more, let alone the likes of me."

But her cynicism couldn't diminish the happiness welling up in her. The dream had been so real that for a few precious moments, it had been almost like having Adam with her.

She hadn't seen her son in thirty years. Thirty lonely, barren years. First she'd lost Jim, then Adam. But the circumstances had been different, she reminded herself. She'd had no control over losing Jim. Not so with Adam. She'd deliberately turned away from Adam. Her son. Her only child. Oh, God, She hadn't meant it to be that way.

From the day they met, Jim had taken care of Allegra's every need, and when he died she found herself unable to function at all. For weeks after his death she lay in bed, staring at the ceiling. Although exhausted, sleep eluded her; she was denied that sweet oblivion. And when a patch of needed sleep finally came, it was fitful, haunted by nightmares. Her waking moments were equally unbearable.

Adam was a constant reminder of her loss. A stirring in her heart had told her he needed her, but she was empty. She had nothing to give. Confused and hurting, she turned her back on her son and sent him away . . .

"Why can't I stay with you, Mom?" ten-year-old Adam had asked tearfully.

Allegra's icy fingers touched her brow. "Because, Adam. I need time to adjust to your father's . . . passing. I . . . I need to be alone, to think." She turned around and leaned her head against the cool pane of the window to distract herself from the pain in her son's eyes. "I'm dead inside, Adam," she sobbed. "I don't know what to do. I don't know where to go. I just don't seem to know anything anymore."

"I'll stay out of your way, Mom." Adam's voice was trembling.

"No," Allegra snapped, feeling hysteria rising. "I don't want you here right now. It's better if you go away to school." She ran her tongue over dry lips and in a strained voice continued, "There will be other boys your age. It'll be more normal for you. Once I get back to work I'll be busy all day at the studio, or traveling, going on location. You know how it is. You'll do fine at school. And I'll send you money."

"You'll come see me?" Adam asked, tears now streaming down his pale little face.

Allegra nodded. "Of course I'll come to see you. We'll spend school vacations together . . ." Her voice trailed off as the memory of her last vacation with Jim came rushing back.

They'd left Adam with Allegra's sister, Stella, and she and Jim flew to Acapulco. He'd never pampered her more than on that glorious vacation. Breakfast in bed every morning. A new outfit delivered to the hotel every afternoon for their night out on the town. Jim arranged for manicures, pedicures, and massages. Allegra felt like a queen.

She knew she could never repay Jim for his thoughtfulness and generosity—she could only love him with all her heart. And she did.

Lying on the bed one evening listening to the waves crashing against the rocks below, Allegra was lulled into a dreamlike state. Jim turned off the air conditioner and opened the balcony windows, then came back to bed. The warm, gentle breeze caressed her body and, closing her eyes, she reached for his hand.

In the distance she heard the strumming of guitars and a chorus of male voices singing Mexican love songs. The music seemed to get louder, and closer. Throwing on a long, silky robe, Allegra walked to the window. Below the balcony stood a group of four musicians. The leader looked up and saluted her.

Allegra was being serenaded.

Coming up behind her, Jim wrapped his arms around her shoulders and Allegra leaned back into his body. Nuzzling her neck, he whispered, "Do you like your serenade, *señora?*"

"You incredible romantic, I love it!" she cried, turning and burying her head in his shoulder.

The day they left Acapulco to return to California, Jim presented Allegra with a recording of the serenade, a souvenir of their ten days in paradise.

But his father's gone now, Allegra had thought sadly as Adam grasped her hand, his eyes so much like Jim's, begging her not to send him away.

Poppy

Allegra looked at her son and for just a moment she wavered. But in the end she held to her decision. She had convinced herself that Adam *would* be better off at a boarding school in Switzerland. She closed her heart to his pleading eyes. So ten-year-old Adam James Walsh walked dejectedly out of her life. Had Allegra only known then that dealing with Adam's loss would be a hundred times more devastating than dealing with Jim's, she never would have sent her son away. By the time she realized her mistake, Adam was lost to her.

Allegra stared at the striped hospital wall, choking back tears. Over the years she'd learned to keep her emotions in check, fearing her heart would break if she set them free.

Then without warning the built-up tears held at bay for thirty-eight years spilled over and a flood, impossible to stop, coursed down her face. Streaking. Soaking. Not breaking her heart as she'd feared, but cleansing her guilt-ridden soul.

"Dear God," Allegra prayed aloud, "is there a chance that I'll see Adam again before I die? Was Poppy right? Were you giving me a sign? Telling me that Adam might find it possible to forgive me?" Suddenly Allegra's heart was open and loving and full.

Wiping the tears away with a tissue from the

pocket of her gown, she sighed. A deep peace descended upon her, a peace she had never known before, not even with Jim.

Allegra slept through dinner and on through the night, amazed when she woke and found it was six o'clock the next morning.

Betty cheerfully entered the room to take her patients' temperatures and let them know breakfast was on the way.

Tillie began her usual chatter, but Allegra wasn't paying attention. She was thinking about how breakfast had been when Jim was alive. How exciting a simple meal could be when shared with her husband.

When their schedules permitted, they'd have breakfast in bed together. Jim insisted on first class treatment—from their finest china and silverware right down to imported Irish linen napkins.

Allegra's eyes clouded over as she lost herself in memory.

Always the romantic, Jim never failed to have a single yellow rose on the silver tray. In the spring, there'd be lilacs as well—but always the rose. The rose was a symbol of his everlasting love for Allegra.

"What pretty gardenias," Betty exclaimed, breaking in on Allegra's reverie. "Did you have a special visitor?"

The old woman smiled. "A friend took me out to the garden by the fountain yesterday and she picked them for me," Allegra said wistfully, remembering her dream of Adam.

"Garden? Fountain?"

"Yes, on the other side of the hospital . . ." Allegra's voice trailed off at the nurse's perplexed expression.

"We do have beautiful grounds with lots of grass and some trees. Yes, I *guess* you could call it a garden," Betty said as she placed the thermometer in her patient's mouth.

There *is* a garden, Allegra said silently. Poppy took me there. She glanced at the gardenias her little friend had placed in the glass, their heady fragrance filling the room. There has to be a garden . . .

Betty checked the thermometer before clearing Allegra's table for the breakfast tray. "Have a good day, you two," she rang out as she left.

Allegra turned her head to the empty wall. The wonderful peace she'd had the night before was gone. If there wasn't a garden, there wasn't a dream, either. So much for God talking and giving signs! Cautiously Allegra again looked at the gardenias Poppy had picked for her. She smiled. For if the flowers were real then her beautiful dream of Adam must be real. Suddenly she felt as if she were destined

to see her son again and when she did the peacefulness would come back to her, this time to stay.

But Allegra's smile faded. The memory of
Adam's face the last time she'd seen him destroyed
any hope of peace. The bright spring afternoon of
his graduation from boarding school in Switzerland
had been the first time she'd seen her son since the
day she'd sent him away. It was also the last.

Allegra had resumed her career within a year
after Jim's death. She was in as much demand as she
had been before the tragedy. Even so, her life had
changed drastically. She was no longer the beloved,
pampered wife. Unable to cope on her own, Allegra
went from one affair to another, looking for someone to love her and take care of her as Jim had done.
But the men in her life were interested only in the
publicity they got from bedding a beautiful, famous
movie star. She sank lower and lower until she was
taking bennies for pick-ups and tranquilizers to
bring herself down. Although outwardly young and
beautiful, she felt decadent.

Afraid to face her son, afraid he would see
through the glamour to the ugliness, Allegra never
once visited Adam at school. When holidays rolled
around she was either on location or in the middle
of rehearsals—always unable to break away from her
schedule, always unable to visit her son. Adam spent

holidays and summer vacations with his European school friends. When Allegra's sister Stella asked Adam to spend some of his vacations with her, he refused. Allegra assuaged her conscience by plying him with lavish gifts and a large checking account. Even though she made sure Adam never wanted for anything material, she never once thought about his emotional needs.

As Allegra approached middle age, the fear of growing old alone overwhelmed her. For the first time in eight years she realized she needed her son. In her vanity, she was sure he would be glad to see her.

She decided to surprise him and fly to Switzerland for his graduation, telling no one of her plans. She wanted their reunion to go unobserved—not splashed all over countless movie magazines.

At the outdoor graduation ceremony, her white, wide-brimmed hat fluttered in the breeze, and she nervously smoothed the white silk dress over her crossed legs, wondering if her fringed red shawl was a little flamboyant for the conservative parents attending the service. But those thoughts vanished as the graduates began walking down the aisle and taking their seats.

Though she hadn't seen Adam for eight years, she would have known him anywhere. As he walked slowly, keeping step with the stately music, a band tightened around her heart. He looked just like Jim—tall, blond and handsome. Would the hurt never go away? Well, she'd have to suppress it today. Today was the beginning of a new relationship with her son. It had taken courage for her to straighten out her life and come here. She wasn't going to let anything mar this wonderful day.

After the ceremony, Allegra hurried to the hall where the party was being held. For a brief moment she wanted to run away, leave without talking to Adam, but she fought down the impulse. She was here now. Everything would be fine. The hardest part was over.

Allegra searched the maze of caps and gowns for her son until she spotted him standing alone, leaning against the wall. Making her way through the crowd, she smiled brightly as she approached him.

"Hello, Adam."

Steely blue eyes locked with hers. "What are you doing here?"

Allegra recoiled as if she'd been slapped. "I came to see you. To congratulate you."

"You've got to be kidding. You tore yourself away from one of your boyfriends long enough to fly all the way to Europe for my graduation?" Adam asked contemptuously.

"I don't think I deserve that kind of talk."

"You don't? What kind of talk does a mother deserve who sends her kid away right after he's lost his father? A mother who sends extravagant presents on birthdays and Christmas but can't ever manage to be there? A mother who sleeps with anything in pants and doesn't care if it's in all the magazines and newspapers? Tell me, what kind of talk do you think you deserve?" Adam's voice trembled with unshed tears.

"I know I did things wrong and I'm sorry. I want to make it up to you." People jostled against them and Adam motioned her to follow him outside.

Once they were alone again, his venomous tirade continued. "Make it up to me? You couldn't possibly make it up to me. Eight years with no mother and no father can't be made up. You think you can make up for all the nights I cried for you to come get me? The times I thought I had done something to kill Dad and you blamed me for it? The years of counseling to rid myself of a guilt that wasn't mine? A guilt caused by you and your self-ishness? It wasn't until I started reading about all your cheap affairs that I realized I had just been in your way. *That's* why you sent me away, not because I had done anything wrong."

"You weren't in my way. I . . . I wasn't prepared to take care of myself, let alone a ten-year-old child. Your father's death devastated me. I had to deal with my grief. I had to find myself."

"And how many beds did you look in? Ten? A hundred? Two hundred?"

Allegra's hand shot out and slapped his face.

Adam's blue eyes narrowed to slits and he glared at her. "I hate you, Allegra Alexander. I hate you more than you can ever know." His voice was cold as ice. "You don't belong here and I don't want you here. So why don't you get on the next plane and get out of my life?"

"But Adam, I'm your mother . . ." Allegra cried, reaching for his arm.

He jerked away from her. "I don't have a mother."

Allegra stiffened as if she'd taken a physical blow. Lifting her head, her teeth clenched to keep her chin from quivering, she turned and walked away. The echo of Adam's words followed her. When she finally reached her rented car, she turned, half-expecting to see her son coming after her. But the parking lot was empty. Just as she was empty.

As the full impact of Adam's words registered, Allegra put her hand over her mouth to smother a soul-wrenching wail. In a daze, she climbed into the car and drove aimlessly for hours. At last, exhausted, she pulled off the road and laid her head on the steering wheel, and felt a numbness settle in her heart.

Allegra was never the same after that. She never shed a tear for what might have been. Instead, she locked her feelings and memories deep inside herself and the hurt grew, silently festering over the years.

Five

Allegra lay back, her gaze riveted to the third pink stripe of the wallpaper until it blended into the white stripe, blurring to a pale pink. She needed to think, to finally sort things out. For three decades she had been an empty shell. Adam's vicious words had haunted her over the years, tearing at the open wound.

At first she blamed the men in her life for keeping her from seeing Adam when he was at school. But she was too intelligent to continue that self-delusion for long. Her own selfishness had kept her from Adam.

He had been right about the many beds she'd looked in trying to find herself. And it had always been the same. Once the glamour of the affair wore off, Allegra felt tainted and cheap. But then a new dalliance would appear on the horizon, waiting, and she would fall into the same trap. After a while, she stopped counting.

By the time Allegra decided to take charge of her life and surprise Adam at his graduation, she was forty-one. Still beautiful, still a top Hollywood star. After eight horrendous years she finally felt in control, able for the first time to make mature decisions. The pills and men who had temporarily filled her life with glitter and excitement after Jim's death were no longer needed. With Adam back in her world, life could start to be good again. A new and vibrant Allegra was emerging.

Unfortunately, when she went to see Adam she was still deluding herself that she was innocent of abandoning her child. Perhaps if she had been able to be honest with him—and herself—that awful day might have turned out differently. Though she was devastated by Adam's accusations, she'd realized the terrible truth of his words. By then, it was too late. He was lost to her again, this time forever.

Allegra blinked, her mind rapidly formulating a plan.

"I'll be darned if I'll give up on Adam," she declared to the empty hospital room. "When Poppy comes I'll have her take me to a phone booth." She glanced at Tillie's bed. "I don't want that chatterbox listening in on my conversation. Or any of the nurses for that matter." She nodded vigorously and a sly grin spread across her face. "Like it or not Adam James Walsh, Allegra Alexander is still your mother!"

Satisfied, Allegra relaxed. Deep in thought, she didn't hear Tillie enter the room. The other woman spoke. "Guess what? I'm leaving today."

"You are?" Allegra asked, instantly alert.

"Uh huh. The doctor told me I could continue my therapy as an outpatient. You know, I'm going to miss you, Allegra."

"*Me*? You're going to *miss* me?" Allegra asked incredulously.

"You're not really all that bad, you know. The last day or so you were even pleasant at times. You must be feeling better, huh?" Tillie said, winding her hair around a curler.

"Well, yes, as a matter of fact, I do feel better— much better, thank you."

"Good. You're too young to be an old crab."

Allegra's hearty laughter echoed through the room. "You know what, Tillie? You're right! You're absolutely right!"

After Tillie said her long, drawn out good-bye with promises to write and visit, Allegra closed her eyes. All these changes, she thought, before dozing off.

Poppy

"Are you sleeping?" Poppy's cheerful voice broke through Allegra's slumberous haze.

"Not anymore," the old woman replied gruffly, suppressing a smile.

"Well, gosh, nobody should sleep all day long," Poppy said, carrying in her guitar and propping it against the chair.

"May I ask why not? What else is there to do around this godforsaken place?"

"There's lots to do and God has not forsaken this hospital," Poppy answered soberly.

"I know. I know. Spare me the lecture," Allegra said with a wave. Struggling to a sitting position, she continued, "I need you to do me a favor, child. I want to make a private phone call later. Can you take me to a phone booth away from the nurses' station after visiting hours?"

"Sure. Are you going to call Adam?"

Allegra gasped, unnerved by the thought that this child could read her mind. "How did you know?"

Poppy shrugged. "It was easy. You just had a dream about him. Remember?"

With a sigh of relief, Allegra said, "Of course I remember," and then motioned to the guitar. "What's this? Are we going to have another concert?"

Poppy

Poppy nodded. "I wrote a song just for you."

Looking at the sweet smile on the little girl's face, Allegra softened. "Let's hear it then, child. But don't make it too loud and cause a commotion."

Poppy smothered a laugh and picked up her guitar. With a dreamy, faraway look in her eyes, she began singing:

Love is the answer
Love paves the way
Forgive those who've hurt you
Forgive them today.
Love is the healer
Love is the key
To unlock the cold heart
That yearns to be free.
Love is Allegra
Allegra is love
God looks upon her
And smiles from above.

Poppy glanced up and saw Allegra silently nodding in agreement, so she repeated the last stanza.

A brilliant smile suddenly lit the old woman's face, washing away years. "Come here, child," Allegra motioned to Poppy.

The little girl leaned the guitar on the chair and

knelt beside the lowered bed in front of the actress. Allegra reached out and caught Poppy's face between her hands, smoothing back her fiery hair. "Do you really believe those words? About love—and forgiving—and God looking down on me and smiling?"

"Oh, yes. I know God loves you. And so does Adam."

Allegra's blue eyes clouded. "How can you be so sure?"

"About God?"

Allegra nodded. "And Adam."

"I just know. There are some things I can't explain; I just know them. And I know that Adam loves you. Just as you love him. There's a bond between a mother and child that's like golden threads woven from one to the other. They can stretch as high and wide as a rainbow," Poppy formed an arc with her outstretched hand, "but they never break."

Allegra released Poppy's face and the girl sat back on her heels. "Oh, I hope you're right, child, I hope you're right."

"I am. You'll see," the little girl answered, scrambling to her feet and retrieving her guitar. "What time do you want to make the call?"

"Come back about eight-thirty, if you can," Allegra said.

"I'll be here," Poppy answered and walked to the door. Then, as if an afterthought, she turned and said, "Do you want the drapes closed?"

"What! And block out that beautiful sunshine! Don't be silly, child. Leave them open."

An impish grin softened Allegra's face and the significance of her words hung in the air. Poppy smiled happily, wearing the expression of someone who had just won a major victory.

"Don't gloat, child. Tomorrow I just may want the room in total darkness again," Allegra said, turning to fluff her pillows.

The little girl's expression never changed. "See you later," she sang from the doorway.

The old woman smiled at the closing door. She was really becoming attached to that child. Poppy was so wise, so knowing, that sometimes—no, oftentimes—it frightened Allegra. She had vowed to find out about her little friend, yet something always prevented her from asking Poppy questions. Am I afraid of the answers? she wondered. Am I afraid that the child might be a figment of my imagination? That, in reality, Poppy doesn't exist? Allegra sighed deeply.

Well, whether Poppy was real or imagined, she needed her. Tears welled in Allegra's eyes as she realized how long it had been since she had needed anyone. Or since anyone had needed her. Did Poppy need her? A stirring inside her heart told her that in some mysterious way the child did, that somehow the two of them were bound together for reasons Allegra was not yet able to fathom. But she was convinced that someday she would know and understand.

With a sinking feeling in the pit of her stomach, she realized that soon she'd have to explain to Poppy about her illness; it wasn't fair to keep it from her. But not yet, she told herself. She couldn't bear to see the child sad and Poppy would be when Allegra told her. The old woman turned her face to the window and stared beyond. It was ironic that with all the people who had adored her over the years, there was now only one who cared whether she lived or died. A little girl.

At exactly eight-thirty, true to her word, Poppy walked into the room. "I found a pay phone at the end of the hall, away from the nurses' station. It'll be real private," Poppy said as she pushed the wheelchair next to the bed. "And I got a bunch of quarters. I knew you'd need change."

"Oh, dear, I forgot all about that. It's a good thing one of us is thinking. Here, help me into this contraption," Allegra said and leaned on Poppy's arm. "Why they insist on these cumbersome wheel-chairs is beyond me. I'm not dying yet," she mumbled.

"Ready?" Poppy asked.

"You're driving, child, so let's get this show on the road."

"Yes, ma'am," she saluted.

Allegra was visibly nervous by the time they stopped in front of the phone booth. She tried un-successfully to keep her hands from shaking. "I'm too far away from the phone, child. You'll have to dial for me."

"Do you ever call Adam?" Poppy asked, her gray eyes burning into Allegra's.

"No. I was afraid to. I . . . I couldn't han-dle another rejection from him," she answered softly.

"And now?"

"There comes a time when some things have to be faced no matter what. For me, that time is now. I have to see Adam once more before . . ." but Allegra's voice broke and she didn't finish the sentence.

Poppy placed her hand on her shoulder. Allegra's wrinkled hand closed over Poppy's small, smooth one and she whispered Adam's number. Standing on tiptoe, the young girl dropped some coins into the slot, listened for a few moments, and handed the phone to Allegra.

"It's ringing," Poppy said.

Allegra took the phone and held it to her ear.

"Hello. Who am I speaking to?" she asked the woman who answered. "Oh, Maggie. You must be Adam's wife. May I speak to him please?"

"May I ask who's calling?" Maggie said pleasantly.

"Who's calling?" Allegra echoed. "Oh! Well, of course you wouldn't know. This is Allegra Alexander . . . Adam's mother."

There followed an interminable silence. Then Maggie answered softly "I'll see if he's available. Will you hold the line please?"

"Yes, I'll hold."

"What's happening?" Poppy whispered.

Putting her hand over the mouthpiece, Allegra answered nervously, "His wife's calling him to the phone."

"Allegra?" Maggie's voice came back on the line. "I'm afraid he's unable to come to the phone. I'm sorry."

"Why is he unable to come to the phone? Is he sick or something?"

"No, no he's not sick. He . . . it's just that . . ." Maggie's deep sigh echoed in Allegra's ear. "I might as well be honest with you. He doesn't want to talk to you," she said sadly. "He said both his parents died when he was ten. I'm terribly sorry . . ."

Allegra dropped the phone and turned her ashen face to Poppy. She hadn't thought it was possible that her heart could break again, but it was shattering into a million fragmented pieces.

"Your God isn't smiling down at me, child, He's laughing," Allegra cried bitterly, and then slumped forward.

Six

Poppy pulled Allegra's head back and bent down to put the old woman's arm around her shoulder. Holding her upright as best she could, she pushed the wheelchair back to the room. Allegra moaned, a sad sound wrenched from her heart.

"Hang on, Allegra," Poppy said, "we're almost there."

Almost there? Where is there? the actress wondered. She stared stonily straight ahead. She felt cold, so very cold. Why didn't she just die? Get it over with once and for all. Why must she go through the motions of living year after year? It was all so useless. Her life was useless. She was useless.

What kind of God would play such terrible tricks on her? Tears ran unchecked down her wrinkled cheeks. Don't be a fool, she chided herself. There is no such thing as God. There is no such thing as love. It's all a mirage. You think it's there, but when you reach out, it disappears—fades away into nothingness. Why couldn't she herself fade away? Was that so much to ask?

"Come on, I'll help you get into bed," Poppy said, yanking the sheet back. Allegra let herself be half-dragged and pulled into bed by the young child.

The little girl wore a worried expression on her face and frowned as she studied Allegra. "We have to talk," she said, tucking the sheet around the old woman.

Allegra's voice sounded as if it had come from far away. "There's nothing to talk about. I should never have let you convince me there was a chance to make amends with Adam. How could I make amends with someone who doesn't exist?"

"Allegra, that's just crazy. Of course Adam exists. What did his wife say to you? What happened?" Poppy asked as she sat down on the bed and began smoothing Allegra's hair from her face.

"You mean you don't know? Why, you're the one who knows everything! How did you miss out on this one?" Allegra asked cruelly, pushing Poppy's hand away. "And to think I was beginning to attribute some sort of . . . some sort of . . . of sainthood to you. But you're just a nosy little girl who likes to meddle in other people's business."

"I wish I could take some of your hurt away," Poppy said softly.

Before Allegra could answer, two nurses rushed in and with hardly a glance in her direction mumbled an apology and pulled the curtain around her bed, blocking her view of the rest of the room.

"Move her next to the bed," a young woman's voice ordered from across the room. "Good. Now help me get her up. Easy." A deep moan and the sound of rustling sheets drifted through the curtain. "Careful," the same competent voice said. "There. She should sleep for a while. Wish we had a private room for her, but this is the only bed available."

"Who's going to monitor her?"

"Jean." Allegra heard a deep sigh. "Such a young thing. It really is too bad about . . ." The door closed and the voice faded out of earshot.

"Open the curtain," Allegra ordered. "If they think I'm going to be stuck in this contraption they call a bed with a shroud wrapped around me, they're crazy!"

But when Poppy pushed the covering aside, they saw that a curtain had been pulled around the other bed, giving the new occupant privacy. They listened for a few moments, but there was only silence. "I guess she's sleeping," Allegra said and turned to Poppy.

"Pull that chair over here and come sit by me," Allegra instructed. When the child was seated in front of her, the old woman reached out and stroked the little girl's silken hair. "You know I didn't mean what I said earlier." Allegra studied Poppy's face. "At least not the part about you. I did mean the rest. Jim is dead. Adam is dead. God is dead. And I want to die, too," she said dully.

"Oh phooey." Poppy pushed the chair back and moved to the bed. "Adam is alive. God is alive. And so are you. You can't give up just because Adam didn't come to the phone today. Give him time to get used to the idea that you want to see him. He was probably in shock."

"I'm tired of fighting, child. I'm tired of being hurt. I'm just plain tired of living," Allegra said solemnly. "There's nothing or no one to live for."

"You live for yourself, that's who you live for. No one can live for someone else. It puts too much strain on the other person. I don't under . . ."

Poppy's words were cut off by a mournful wail. She and Allegra stared round-eyed at the blank curtain, but now there was only silence. And then they heard soft cries and moans coming from the other side of the thin material.

Shuddering, Allegra nudged Poppy toward the other bed. She walked quietly over and listened. A few minutes later she nodded to Allegra and whispered, "Sounds like she's okay now."

As Poppy turned away, the young woman's frantic voice cut through the silence. "My legs . . . hurt . . ."

Poppy gave Allegra a quick glance and opened the curtain. She looked down at a young woman no more than twenty years old. Wild brown eyes stared straight ahead. Then her head began to thrash about frantically.

Poppy's glance moved from the pain-glazed face down the slim body and over the tented sheet. She turned quickly to Allegra, who shook her head.

"I'll ring for the nurse," Allegra said, reaching for the call button.

Poppy headed for the door, but stopped when Allegra, in a pleading voice, asked, "You're coming back, aren't you?

"Did you think I wouldn't?" She smiled sweetly.

"Well, after all the things I said a few minutes ago I wouldn't blame you if you decided not to," the old woman whispered.

"It would take more than words spoken from a broken heart to keep me away. Besides, I adopted you as my grandmother, remember?" Her voice took on a teasing, playful tone. "I'm afraid you're stuck with me."

Tears glistened in Allegra's eyes. "I've never had a granddaughter, but you've given me more warmth and happiness in the little time I've known you than I've had in many, many years. Thank you, child."

Poppy's enormous gray eyes absorbed Allegra's hurt. "I love you, Allegra," she said softly and blew a kiss across the room.

The simple, childish act completely disarmed the old woman. In that instant she realized she loved Poppy as if she were her own. Her feelings hadn't been stripped away by the phone call after all. But these thoughts could wait. Right now she had to get help for the young patient beside her. She pushed the call button again. Longer this time.

"Yes?" Jean whispered, poking her head in the door.

"The young woman in the other bed—she seemed to be in pain a few minutes ago. She said her legs were hurting, but I think she's fallen asleep now."

"I was just on my way in to monitor her. Poor girl. She doesn't have any legs. They had to amputate from the knees down."

Allegra glanced over at the woman lying beneath the raised sheet. "She was probably delirious."

Jean walked over to her.

"They were in a three-car collision. The baby

wasn't hurt at all. He'd been fastened in his car seat in the back. Her husband, David, wasn't hurt badly, only shaken, but he couldn't get her out. The front of the car was jammed up against her legs. The paramedics freed her, but it took a long time.

"It wasn't until they were in the ambulance that he realized how badly she'd been hurt. Her legs were crushed beyond repair. They had to be amputated."

"She doesn't know yet?" Allegra asked softly.

"No. She just got out of ICU and she's still sedated."

"She's so young—and pretty." Allegra thought of her own youth. "What's her name?"

"Sara Michaels. She was a model before she had her baby. It's going to be real hard on her. Her whole life has changed in a matter of hours," Jean said ruefully as she lifted the limp hand to monitor the sleeping woman's pulse.

Allegra knew that when Sara discovered her legs were gone, it would be worse than her life being *changed*. Unless she were an extremely strong person, it would be more than the beautiful girl could face. She had seen actresses under less trauma fall apart and never recover.

"They're sure the baby and her husband are okay?" Allegra asked.

"The baby's fine. Not a scratch on him. As I

said, her husband was shaken up. But not too badly. He was treated and sent home. I'd appreciate it if you'd ring me when she wakes up." Allegra nodded and Jean left the room.

The curtains had been left open and Allegra lay there watching Sara's face, now peaceful in sleep. She wondered if it would be enough for Sara to know that her husband and baby were unhurt in the accident.

The young woman didn't cry out again and eventually Allegra fell asleep.

Early the next morning Sara's doctor came into the room and, nodding a perfunctory greeting to Allegra, swished the curtain briskly around her bed, shutting her out. She knew immediately that he was going to tell Sara about her legs. Allegra was relieved to be cloistered. She didn't want to be part of anyone else's heartaches; she'd had enough of her own. Still she couldn't help overhearing the doctor talking to Sara, trying to soothe her as he told her the truth.

The anguished cry that ripped through the room was unlike anything Allegra had ever heard. The doctor called for his nurse and they tried to calm Sara, but she kept screaming and the doctor ordered an injection.

"I won't live without legs, do you hear? I'm

going to die and you won't be able to stop me," Sara screamed hysterically before the sedative took effect.

"Call her husband," the doctor instructed the nurse.

Allegra lay in her bed shaking, grateful for her curtain cocoon. A little while later she heard footsteps moving toward the other bed and a low, masculine voice say, "Sara, wake up, love. It's David."

There was no answer.

Allegra secluded herself behind the curtain for the day. She picked at her breakfast and lunch, paying little attention to the food. As far as she knew, David continued his vigil all morning.

She dozed off and was awakened by David's pleading voice. "Sara. Please talk to me. Please." His voice broke and there were muffled sobs.

She put her hands over her ears, embarrassed to be intruding on their privacy. But his voice carried across the small room.

"I'm not leaving till you talk to me. Don't you understand, I love you. I know how you feel, but please think of Greg. He's so little. He needs you. And God, so do I, Sara." His voice cracked.

"You don't know how I feel," she answered in a dull, lifeless voice, her words spaced as if she had to think of each one individually. "You still have your legs. I can't spend the rest of my life in a wheel-chair. I can't."

"You're strong, Sara. You'll adjust if you give yourself time."

Her voice strengthened. "I'll never adjust. Never!" Then her voice reverted to the monotone. "I want to be alone now."

David walked to the door. "I'll be back tomor-row," he said, sounding defeated. The door closed softly.

"I'm going to die, David. I've made up my mind to die," Sara whispered.

Allegra couldn't remain silent any longer. "Ex-cuse me," she said through the curtain, "I know it's none of my business, but I can't help being aware of what's going on in this room. You have every-thing to live for. A husband. A baby."

"You're right. It *is* none of your business. And what do you know about any of this? You didn't have to go through life without legs, did you?" Sara sobbed.

"No, I didn't," Allegra answered, turning her face to the window. But I had to go through life without my husband and child, she said silently.

Sara seemed to be getting her wish. She began to go downhill and her doctor couldn't stop the decline.

From her bed, Allegra heard David beg and plead with his wife to fight to live. He even brought the baby into the room, but nothing reached her.

Finally, unable to idly stand by and watch this beautiful girl die, Allegra took action. She sat in the chair by Sara's bed and spoke firmly as the girl remained motionless, staring straight ahead. "Young lady, it's time you stopped wallowing in self-pity and got on with your life. If killing yourself affected only you, then I'd say go ahead. But you've got David to think about. And your baby."

"David needs to find another wife—a whole one with two legs. If he stays with me, in time he'll be ashamed of me. I'm a cripple." Sara stopped and bit her trembling lip. "I can't expect him to be satisfied with half a woman for the rest of his life. It's not fair to him. He deserves more than that." She turned around to face Allegra, tears brimming.

"David loves you, Sara," Allegra said. "*You.* Not your legs. And do you think any other woman in the world is going to love your baby the way you do? Are you so willing to trust him to a stranger?" Allegra's voice cracked and she had to steady herself.

"What do you know about anything? I'm told you were a movie star. Your life is probably perfect."

"It was once," Allegra said softly.

Sara's gaze focused. "Once?"

Allegra found herself doing what she had sworn she would never do again—telling the story of her life with Jim and Adam. She left out nothing. She willingly exposed her anguish in a desperate attempt to reach Sara, to force her to accept the gift of life.

Impulsively, Allegra took the beautiful face in her hands, compelling Sara to look at her. "I just have one more thing to say and then I'll leave you alone."

Allegra's gaze locked with Sara's and held it fixed as she whispered, "I would gladly have given my legs if I could have had Jim and Adam again."

Sara reached up and pulled Allegra down to her, clutching the older woman tightly.

Seven

Allegra gently unlocked Sara's arms from her neck and studied the tear-streaked face.

"Thank you, Allegra," Sara said quietly. "Thank you for sharing such an intimate part of your life with me. I know it wasn't easy for you to talk about it. I'd like to be alone now. I . . . I need to think."

Allegra went back to her side of the room and looked out the window. If her story had reached Sara, opened the young woman's eyes to what life was all about, then it had been worth the pain of telling it.

Late that afternoon, Sara called Allegra over. When Allegra was next to the young woman's bed she saw that the anguish was gone. In its place, a soft peace had settled. Allegra smiled.

Tears glistening in her luminous brown eyes, Sara touched Allegra's hand. "I see now how vain and selfish I've been. Will you get the call button for me please? I want to see David and Greg."

Allegra handed her the cord and then walked over to the other side of the room.

A few minutes later Jean poked her head in the doorway. "Who rang?"

"I did," Sara announced proudly. "I want to see my husband and my baby."

The nurse's eyebrows shot up. "Just a minute," she said, hurrying out.

"Does my hair look all right?" Sara asked.

"It's fine. Here. See for yourself." Allegra handed her a mirror. "Do you have lip gloss?"

"I don't know if I have any here."

Allegra rummaged through the drawer beside the young woman's bed. "Here's some."

Sara's fingers lingered on Allegra's as she took the tube from her. "Thank you again. For everything. I feel as if I've been given a new lease on life. I guess I have, haven't I? I hope I don't mess it up."

Allegra patted Sara's hand. "It won't be easy, dear. There will probably be times when you'll wish you hadn't listened to me. But if you can just concentrate on the joy you can give your husband and Greg—and the joy you'll get in return watching your son grow up, you'll do just fine."

"And if that fails, I'll remember you." Sara's large brown eyes misted.

Allegra sighed. "How much easier life would be if we really *could* learn from other people's mistakes. But most of us have to make our own. Foolish. Very foolish," she ended in a whisper.

Sara chewed her bottom lip. "Do you think David still wants me? I mean . . . I've been so heartless," she said worriedly.

"Of course he still wants you. And you weren't being heartless. You were fighting something you had no control over."

The young woman's gaze rested on Allegra's face. "Do you really think so?"

"Yes, I do." Allegra squeezed Sara's hand, wanting so much to help her.

"Allegra?" Sara asked hesitantly.

"Yes?"

Sara pointed to the shiny red apple on the table. "Could I have that apple? I'm starving!"

Allegra laughed and handed it to her. "I'll ring the nurse and have her bring something to eat."

"Thanks," Sara mumbled, her words garbled by the mouthful of fruit.

Jean poked her head in the room. "You rang?"

"Yes," Allegra answered. "Our little friend here is hungry."

"I'll see what I can do," Jean said, looking carefully at Sara and nodding.

A few minutes later the portly nurse came back with a tray. "This is all I could round up but dinner'll be ready soon and I'll make sure you're served first." She stopped at the door. "By the way, Sara. Your husband said he was going to pick up Greg and they'll be here shortly." She smiled and left the room.

"Oh, Allegra," Sara wailed, "I think I've lost my appetite."

"Well, eat anyway. You need your strength," Allegra counseled.

Less than half an hour later the door opened and David walked in carrying the baby. He hesitated at the door.

Sara looked up and reached out to him. "David, oh, David, I'm so sorry. So very, very sorry," she cried.

In an instant he was at her side, balancing the baby with one arm as he covered his wife's face with kisses, their tears mingling.

"I have good news for you," Jean called from the door. "We have a vacant private room and the doctor left orders for you to be moved." Turning to David, she added, "That means you can visit whenever you want. You won't have to worry about visiting hours. And it's all right to bring the baby. We'll just turn our backs as you come and go." She smiled.

"Thank you," David answered.

"Let me have Greg," Sara said, holding out her arms for the baby.

Allegra turned her head to the window, torn between her happiness for the young family and her own pain of losing Adam.

Later, as Sara was wheeled out of the room, she waved good-bye and Allegra's spirits plummeted. Alone again. How she hated being alone. Allegra wondered if Sara really knew how blessed she was to have David and her baby. And she might have more children some day. A sigh came from deep inside her.

"Hi! Want some company?"

Turning, Allegra stared at Poppy. "Where have you been, child? I thought I'd been deserted." A stain of pink colored Allegra's cheeks.

"I came by a few times but there was always so much going on in here that I thought I'd better wait till things quieted down." Poppy looked over at the empty bed.

Allegra's gaze followed the girl's. "They moved Sara to a private room so her husband and baby could be with her."

"She's going to be okay?"

Allegra smiled. "I think she will."

"What about you?" Poppy asked, sitting on Allegra's bed and looking at her. "Are you going to be okay?" She tucked her hair behind her ear but it quickly fell over her brow again.

"What do you mean?" Allegra asked.

"I mean when are you going to get on with your life?"

"What in the world are you talking about, child?"

"Do you plan on staying in this hospital forever?" Poppy persisted.

Allegra studied Poppy, wondering how much she should tell the child. No, not yet, she thought. "I'll stay until Dr. Morgan tells me I can leave."

"But don't you want to get out of here?"

The old woman turned away and didn't answer.

"Well, don't you, Allegra?" Poppy insisted.

"It doesn't make any difference one way or the other." Allegra motioned with her hand. "An empty house. An empty hospital room."

Poppy touched the old woman's arm. "But, Adam—"

"You were there when I called him," Allegra snapped. "Adam doesn't . . . " She sucked in her breath and clenched her fists tightly until her knuckles whitened. Her eyes shut, she tried to blot out the sudden stab of pain.

"Allegra? What is it? What's the matter?" Poppy asked anxiously.

Allegra started to wave the little girl away, then stopped. Looking into Poppy's eyes, gray as a foggy night, Allegra saw wisdom and compassion too profound for such a young child.

She clutched at Poppy's hands and pulled her closer, knowing she had to tell her now. It couldn't wait any longer. "I have a malignant tumor, child. Dr. Morgan told me the pain will get worse and more frequent. He told me to get my affairs in order because I have only six months—possibly a year— to live." Allegra turned her face into the pillow.

"Allegra, listen to me. Doctors are not God! They can't tell a person how long she has to live. You know, faith can work miracles." She put her arms around the old woman and hugged her. "Not always. But many times," she whispered.

"I'm afraid I don't have the kind of faith miracles are made of," Allegra said.

"How do you know?"

"Because I'm not sure I even believe in God anymore."

"But He believes in you. That's what's important. He's always there. We just have to turn ourselves around. He never leaves us. It's we who leave Him," Poppy said, her eyes gleaming with light.

"How do you know so much, child?"

Poppy shrugged. "I just know."

A sigh rose from deep within Allegra. "I'm too worn out, child. It would be easier to just give up . . ."

"Only quitters talk like that."

"Don't you see? I'm tired of fighting. After Jim died I had to fight to stay at the top. But I lost so much—my dignity, my self-respect. Worst of all, I lost Adam. Oh, it was an expensive fight. And not worth it *at all*." She turned her face away to hide her shame.

"You mustn't be bitter. You can't undo the past. But you can mend the present."

"It's too late to mend anything. I can't even mend myself. I'm dying, child. Don't you understand?"

Wise gray eyes locked with somber blue ones.

"Yes, I understand."

"I'm sorry, child. I don't mean to take my frustrations out on you. But I have no one else to talk to. No one else to tell how afraid I am. I don't want to lie here feeling sorry for myself. But I can't seem to help it." Allegra's deep sobs filled the room.

Poppy slid her arms around Allegra's slumped

shoulders and rocked her back and forth. In a reversal of roles, the young child became the comforter, the old woman the comforted.

Allegra's tears gradually subsided. "You're a sweet child to put up with the ravings of a has-been old actress," she said, straightening herself. "I've been acting so long I can't tell if it's really me anymore or if it's a role I'm playing."

Poppy walked to the window and closed the drapes. She propped Allegra up with pillows and sat on the bed again.

"You're not the same person you were then. You've suffered too much and searched too long. You're beyond play-acting. The time you have left is for real. Every minute counts—whether you live six months, six years, or six millennia."

"And how do I make each minute count?" the aging woman asked.

"Well, you start by forgiving."

"Adam?"

Poppy nodded. "And yourself."

Allegra shook her head. "I don't think I can," she whispered.

"There must be forgiveness before you can make your peace with God."

Allegra scowled. "Who said I wanted to make peace with God?" she asked indignantly.

"How else can every minute count?" Poppy answered matter-of-factly.

"For someone so young, you sure have a way with words. You should be a lawyer when you grow up."

Poppy smiled and shrugged.

"Well, you really ought to. But first you'll have to get that mop of hair cut so it doesn't keep flopping in your eyes. If you don't go into law, I think you'll be missing your calling," Allegra remarked dryly.

"We never miss our calling, Allegra. Sometimes we don't know what it is right away, but sooner or later we find out. And when we do, we have to follow it."

"And was my calling to be a movie star?" Allegra asked in a mocking voice.

"That's just your profession. Your calling hasn't come yet."

"I'm too old to take on anything new now."

"Spiritually we are all ageless. No one is ever too old to answer God's call."

Allegra studied the girl. "I've been calling you *child*, but you're not a child, are you?"

Poppy's eyes widened.

"You have a wise and infinite mind in a child's body. I don't understand it but I can feel it." Allegra nodded. "I need time to mull over all this wisdom you've been pouring into me."

"It's just a way of life. The way to be happy and bring happiness to others. Isn't that what you told Sara?"

Allegra's gaze snapped up and she peered at Poppy keenly. "How do you know what I told Sara?"

"I don't for sure. But I have a feeling you helped her decide she wanted to live again. And it's no different for you. Whatever you told her applies to you, too," Poppy reasoned.

"But she's a young woman with her whole life ahead of her. I'm old. She has a husband and son. I have nothing and no one."

"You have a son."

"A son who claims his mother is dead. What kind of son is that?" Allegra asked.

Poppy said softly, "One who needs your love and understanding."

"First it was forgiveness," Allegra said sharply. "Now it's love and understanding."

"It's all of those. You have to love Adam *as he is* and understand his feelings. Then you'll be able to release the pain his words caused you. When you can forgive him, you'll be able to forgive yourself, and then you'll have made your peace with God."

Allegra looked past the window. "I do love Adam. I've always loved him. And I understand why he feels the way he does. Why he refused to come to the phone." She turned back to Poppy. "So why is it so difficult for me to forgive him?"

"Because of ego—our own human nature. You're afraid you'll be hurt again. But we have to push that out of the way and become like little children. Trusting. Loving. Forgiving."

"But I don't know how to do that. Can you help me?" Allegra asked as she reached for Poppy's hand.

The little girl smiled and nodded. "Why don't we pray together?"

"I don't even know how to pray, child. I haven't prayed in years . . ."

"Just close your eyes, and in your mind's eye see yourself and Adam just the way you'd like it to be. Don't just daydream. Feel the emotion of seeing him. Of his arms around you, hugging you. Touch his face. Feel his tears of happiness and wipe them away like you did when he was a child. Hear his voice telling you he loves you. Look into his eyes and know that this is real. Then thank God for answering your prayer."

"But that didn't really happen . . ."

"No, but it will. Just have faith, Allegra, have faith."

The old woman lowered her eyelids and moved her lips silently. A feeling of peacefulness filled her body and she was vaguely aware of Poppy tiptoeing to the door and closing it gently behind her.

Eight

The bright early morning sun awakened Allegra the next day. Poppy must have planned something special, she thought and sat up. A smile warmed her face and she waited impatiently for the little girl to appear. But every time the door opened, it turned out to be either a nurse with a thermometer or Dr. Morgan making rounds. Where was that child? Why wasn't she here?

Allegra suddenly wondered if Poppy might be trying to tell her something by her absence. What an absurd idea. What in the world could a nine-year-old be trying to tell her?

Instantly the previous night flashed before her and Allegra slowly replayed the scene, listening once more to the wisdom of the young child. As the last words faded away, Allegra realized that Poppy had done all she could to help her. It was now up to

Allegra to decide whether she would go on living or give up and die.

Perhaps she wouldn't be able to stretch the six months into six years, but for whatever time she had left she could live fully. Or she could shrivel and die inside long before her body did. Isn't that what she'd been doing? Shriveling and dying slowly under a pretense of living?

Allegra had accused Sara of being selfish. But what about herself? Hadn't she spent years crying over *her* loss after Jim died? Hadn't she felt the victim at Adam's graduation when he'd rejected her? She'd become so wrapped up in feelings of self-pity that she built a wall around herself, a wall that not only protected her but insulated her from hurt and suffering, from life itself.

What was the very worst that could happen to her? Death? No, death wouldn't be the worst. Living? Allegra pondered this for several minutes. Okay, if I live, what would be the worst that could happen? She heard herself whisper aloud, "That I'll never see or hear from Adam."

But you haven't seen or heard from him for thirty years, something inside her answered, *and you went on living.* But not happily, she argued. *Because you chose not to be happy. You chose it!* Is it as easy as that? Allegra wondered. Do I just *choose* to be sad or happy? And if that's the case, do I also choose to be sick or well? To live or slowly die?

Allegra's mind reeled. Conflicting thoughts spun around relentlessly and she could find no answers. She wasn't sure there even were any.

Putting her hands to her head, she rubbed her temples. "Well, if there are so many choices available," she said aloud, "I'm going to make one right now. I'm not staying in this bed another minute. And I'm not letting them shove me into that wheelchair either. From now on, I'm going to walk."

She slid off the bed and walked to the window, leaning against it. As she looked out and watched the slight breeze ruffle the weeping willow, the old woman smiled. Summer was her favorite season. Summer meant beautiful flowers dressed in magnificent colors. Summer meant warm, starlit nights.

Allegra suddenly shivered as her gaze followed a leaf that fluttered to the ground. It reminded her of autumn. She had never liked autumn. She still didn't. She found the season depressing. Autumn meant the end of summer, and though the falling leaves had a beauty of their own, the season still reminded Allegra of death.

Thinking back, she remembered how, as a child living in New York State, she had dreaded the coming of winter. The snow and the ice. And the terrible, terrible cold. She had disliked winter and would hibernate during the frosty months, devouring books. As a youngster she had read every spare moment, but somewhere along the way she had grown away from reading. Now, suddenly, she yearned to read again, not the books of her childhood but books written by masters of life.

She crossed to the door and opened it, carefully making her way to the nurses' station.

Betty looked up from her papers. Her eyes widened. "Why aren't you in a wheelchair?"

"Don't worry. I'm fine. Just fine." Allegra leaned against the counter. "Do you have a library here?"

"Well, no, not a library. But I can get you some magazines, *Reader's Digest* . . ."

"No, no. I want something deeper. Something meaty."

Betty studied her. "You mean like Jackie Collins or Harold Robbins?"

"Not that kind of meaty," Allegra chuckled. "Something about the meaning of life. About love. Forgiveness."

"Love. Oh, yes. I think I can get you a couple of books by Leo Buscaglia. There's one of his that everyone's been reading—*The Fall of Freddie the Leaf.*"

"Is that some kind of kid's book?"

"Not at all. Buscaglia says it's a story of life for all ages. Would you like me to try to find a copy for you?"

Allegra nodded and walked back to her room. She sat down on her bed, eager to begin reading.

Allegra was delighted to see the sprightly young woman nudge the door open with her foot several minutes later, her arms laden with books. She dumped them unceremoniously on the bed.

"These ought to keep you out of trouble for a while," Betty chortled. "You must be feeling pretty good, huh?"

"Yes, I do feel pretty good. And I'm going to feel even better."

"Well, good for you. I hope some of these titles are what you had in mind," she said from the doorway.

Allegra nodded and, reaching for her glasses, rummaged through the books excitedly.

"Wonderful! Corrie Ten Boom's *The Hiding Place*. And look. Anne Lindbergh's *A Gift From the Sea*." Then she picked up a frayed book and opened its cover. "*A Severe Mercy*," she said in a whisper, tears forming in her eyes. "I started reading this a long time ago, but never could make myself finish it. Maybe I can now." She placed it gently on the bed and continued looking through the pile. "Ah, here's *The Fall of Freddie the Leaf.*" Allegra plumped her pillows and picked up the slender book. "I think I'll start with this one."

She read the story twice and found herself staring at the last page—two solitary words—The Beginning.

With the back of her hand, Allegra wiped away a tear. She would read the other books, but she didn't really need them. Her answer had come through Freddie. Suddenly, autumn wasn't a threat anymore, nor was winter. Because she understood now that without them there could be no spring or summer. The whole cycle was part of God's plan for His universe. All of it was necessary. All of it was good. And she, Allegra, was part of it.

Smiling, she lay on the bed and fell asleep, *The Fall of Freddie the Leaf* held lovingly against her breast.

A short time later Allegra awakened and felt a presence in the room. Poppy was standing by the window, her hand on the drapery cord.

"Don't draw them. I just closed my eyes for a few minutes. As you can see," Allegra said, her hand sweeping over the mound of books spread across the bed, "I have a lot of reading to do. And I need to walk around more every day. If I keep lying here in this bed I'll wind up an invalid for sure. That would interfere with my plans."

"Your plans?" Poppy's eyebrows rose.

"All of us were created for a reason. I'm still not sure exactly what mine is, but I do know what it isn't: it isn't to hang around feeling sorry for myself. Somehow I have to be of use, to help people. I don't have the answer yet, but I'm working on it," Allegra said proudly and sat up.

Poppy reached for the book still in Allegra's hand. "Did you learn all that from Freddie?"

Allegra's eyes met Poppy's eyes. "Not all of it, child."

The little girl smiled and said, "Tell me about your plans." She shoved the books aside so she could sit down next to Allegra.

"Well, for one thing, I'm going to get well. As well as God allows. And for however long He gives me, I'm going to spend that time talking with people who think they don't want to live anymore, the way I did with Sara. It's okay to die—we all do—but we must live fully up to that moment. We mustn't stop living before we actually die. Do you understand what I'm trying to say?"

Poppy nodded, her eyes bright with excitement. "You said it very well."

"So I'm going to read to strengthen my mind,

walk to strengthen my body, and pray to strengthen my spirit. And in the not too distant future, I'm going to leave this hospital."

"I'm sure you will. And you'll be a joy and inspiration to everyone you come in contact with." Poppy touched Allegra's hand. "What about Adam?"

The old woman sighed, shaking her head slowly. "I've done everything I could, child. I'm going to have to let it go and put the whole thing in God's hands. My trying to manipulate Adam didn't work so I'm going to turn it over to God."

"And if you two never get together . . . ?"

"You're asking if all my newly formed plans depend on my relationship with Adam, aren't you?"

Poppy nodded.

"Well, as much as I want to be reconciled with my son, I can't let what happened between us destroy the rest of my life. If things don't work out in this life, there will be another time for us."

"Heaven?" Poppy suggested.

The old woman shrugged her thin shoulders. "Something like that."

"Allegra!"

"Okay, okay. Heaven," she said and put her hands up in surrender.

Several days later when the doctor stopped in

to see Allegra, she was wearing the robe Poppy had brought her and was patting her hair into place. Looking up, she smiled cheerfully, "Hello, Dr. Morgan."

"Hello, Allegra." The doctor studied her for a moment, then looked at her chart. "I understand you've stopped taking pain pills."

"I don't need them anymore."

He raised his eyebrows. "Care to tell me why?"

"Pain pills are for pain. I don't have any."

"None?" he asked.

Allegra met his eyes. "Not a twinge."

"And why do you think that is?" The young doctor looked at her attentively.

Allegra shrugged. "You're the doctor," she said good-humoredly.

"Yes," he muttered, trying to hide a smile.

"Well, maybe I do know, doctor," Allegra said as she carefully laid her brush down on the table. "Maybe it has to do with attitudes and beliefs and goals." And trust in a little red-haired girl, she added silently.

"And what are your attitudes and beliefs and goals?" Dr. Morgan asked quietly.

"I decided to get on with my life. I got tired of lying around crying because the world had done me

117

in. I have goals now, doctor. I want to help as many people as I can."

"In what way, Allegra?" Dr. Morgan sat back in the chair and rested his chin on his steepled fingertips.

"The only way I know how. By talking. There are many people in this hospital who feel the way I used to. So I stop by to see them, take them books to read, and talk to them. Some of them respond. And some don't. But more respond than don't, and that's what I have to remember. I like to think I'm an instrument in their healing."

"Healing?" He leaned forward.

"Yes, healing of their mental attitudes."

He nodded. "Well, let's get back to you. How are you feeling, besides not having any pain?"

"Like new. I think I'm ready to leave here," she said.

"Perhaps. But I think we need to do a few more tests on you first. I'd like to take another CAT scan. See how that tumor is looking."

"Suits me. When do you want to do it?"

"I'll schedule it for tomorrow morning at nine. Be sure to get plenty of rest tonight," he said as he rose. He smiled at her warmly before leaving.

She waved him out and promptly forgot the test, lost in the business of visiting other patients.

Poppy

The day Dr. Morgan was to give Allegra her CAT scan results, she stood by the window, her freshly manicured fingernails tapping the windowsill. She was in a hurry to get it over with because she had books to deliver and she didn't want her schedule interrupted.

Allegra turned as the doctor opened the door. He motioned for her to sit down, then pulled a chair up beside her for himself.

He watched her silently for a moment, then said, "I don't know how to tell you this."

For a minute Allegra's heart pounded. Then she reminded herself that the results of the scan wouldn't make any difference. Her life would go on the same way.

She looked the doctor squarely in the eye. "I can take it."

Dr. Morgan smiled. "Oh, I'm sure you can. It's gone."

"What's gone? You lost the test?"

"No, the tumor," he said, taking her hands in his.

"*You lost the tumor?*" she asked incredulously.

Dr. Morgan's eyes were bright with excitement. "The tumor's gone. It's not there anymore. I can't explain it: it's gone into remission."

Allegra's eyes shone. "It's not a remission, doctor. It's a miracle." Thank you, God, she said silently.

"Call it what you want to, but it's vanished." Dr. Morgan watched her for a long moment before getting up and walking to the door. "You'll be happy to know you can leave the hospital in a few days. But first I'd like to do some blood work—just to be sure."

She nodded absently, her thoughts already racing to Poppy. She couldn't wait to tell her the good news. . . . Yet deep in her heart, Allegra was convinced that Poppy already knew.

Nine

Anxious to make plans now that she'd be leaving the hospital in a few days, Allegra reviewed her finances. She still had the money from Jim's life insurance in the bank. Because she had always thought of it as blood money, she'd never touched it. Now she was able to look at the situation more realistically. It was merely a type of barter you received in exchange for something else. Logically she knew that Jim wouldn't have had insurance if he hadn't wanted her to use it.

Allegra slowly walked to the window, her mind busily sorting out details. She didn't need her big, fancy house anymore. She was finished with that. What she needed now was a small, centrally located apartment and a dependable car. She made a mental note to call her lawyer to take care of the details. The rest of her money would go to help people, to buy books and gifts to let them know they were loved.

She stared wistfully out the window and wished somehow that Poppy could . . .

"No, no, no," Allegra said aloud, shaking her head. "This is no time to go soft and sentimental. The child is already pulling away—as if now that she has accomplished her mission, she's getting ready to move on." Allegra twisted the belt of her robe and caught her bottom lip between her teeth. "But where will you go, child?" she whispered to the silent room, tears glistening in her blue eyes. "Where will you go?"

Turning away from the window, Allegra resolutely picked up one of the books lying on the table. She leafed through it but her eyes were unable to focus on the blurred words. The image of Poppy's face covered the page. A moan sounded from deep inside Allegra. She lifted her gaze, overwhelmed by a sense of loss—and the time of parting hadn't even come yet.

With a huge sigh, she removed her robe and climbed into bed, forcing herself to focus on pleasant thoughts. Sara quickly came to mind. The lovely young mother was making a remarkable recovery. How gratifying it was to see her vast improvement after those few words Allegra had given her. At dinner earlier that evening in Sara's room, the young woman had talked constantly about David and Greg and Allegra's heart expanded when she heard the happiness in Sara's voice. I've come a long way, Allegra thought sleepily.

Closing her eyes, she gradually dozed off. A knock on the door startled her awake.

"Come in, come in, child. Since when are you getting formal? You've never knocked before . . ."

Allegra's words trailed off and she covered her mouth with her hand, her eyes widening in disbelief. It wasn't Poppy who opened the door. It was Adam. Am I dreaming? she wondered, shaking her head. Dear Lord, she prayed, please don't let it be a dream. Please let it really be Adam.

"Mother?" Adam asked hesitantly.

Allegra nodded, staring at her son, unable to speak.

He walked toward her, a shy smile on his face. "I'm sorry if I alarmed you. I guess I should have let you know I was coming."

With an effort, she regained her voice. "No, no. That's . . . all right." She motioned for him to sit in the chair by her bed as she fought to keep her hands from shaking. But she couldn't control the tremors within. She had no idea why he was there, but he was—and for the moment that was all that mattered.

"I talked to the doctor before I came in," he said, ignoring the chair and sitting on the edge of her bed.

"Oh?"

"He said you're fine and that you can leave the hospital in a couple of days."

"Yes," Allegra whispered, staring at her son, still so much like Jim. She ached to reach out and hold him close—the way she had when he was young. But she sat erect, quietly waiting for him to speak.

He seemed to be probing every line in her face. "I was wondering what you're going to do when you get out. Where you'll live. . . ." He hesitated. She was puzzled by his question.

"I . . . I'm selling my house and getting a small apartment—nothing big or fancy. Something easy to take care of."

"You shouldn't be living by yourself."

"That's silly," she said with a wave of her hand. "There's nothing wrong with me now. Why shouldn't I live by myself?"

He cleared his throat. "Won't you be lonely?"

Allegra stared at him. I've been lonely for thirty-eight years, she said to herself. Cheerfully she said, "I'm going to get myself a kitten. Might even get a pair." But in the back of her mind she wondered where all this small talk was leading.

As if he'd read her thoughts, Adam whispered, "I'm sorry, Mother."

"Sorry? Why? Because I'm getting two kittens?"

He chuckled. "You used to always do that when I was a kid. Deliberately misunderstand." Haltingly taking Allegra's hands in his, his eyes searched hers. Allegra felt him tremble. "I'm sorry we wasted so many years. I'm sorry for the bitter words—for the mistrust—for the distance between us—for thinking I didn't love you anymore."

"Adam, I . . ." she faltered, wholly unnerved by his touch and the warmth flowing from his hands to hers.

He put his finger against her lips and hushed her. "I wouldn't blame you if you didn't want anything to do with me. I don't deserve anything after the way I treated you at my graduation. And then refusing to talk to you when you called recently . . ."

This is the miracle, Allegra thought. Adam here with me. Even if I die this second, I'll have had this miracle.

"I'm the one," Allegra protested.

"No. You tried to explain: I wouldn't listen. I was too young and bullheaded even to hear you out.

In some ways I can forgive myself for graduation day because I *was* so young. But it's been thirty years and supposedly I've matured. Yet I never made a move to contact you—to listen to your side of the story."

"But that's only because I hurt you so terribly. Your wounds were deep. It wasn't your fault. It was all mine." Tears trickled down her face.

"Please don't cry," he said, wiping the tears away.

"Oh, Adam," Allegra sobbed, crumpling toward him.

He moved swiftly and gently, holding her, their tears mingling.

Raising her head, Allegra saw Poppy standing in the doorway, smiling at them. As their eyes met over Adam's head, Poppy blew a kiss across the room, a kiss that seemed to encircle mother and son. Allegra started to motion the little girl to come into the room but even as Allegra's hand lifted, Poppy disappeared. Suddenly the old woman feared that the child had gone from her life forever.

"What's the matter?" Adam asked as Allegra stiffened.

She wanted to tell him about Poppy, but something stopped her. "Oh, nothing," she answered, pushing thoughts of her little friend aside. She'd have to deal with that later, when she was alone. "Tell me all about your Maggie."

"We've been married twenty-five years and she's the most marvelous woman I've ever met." His voice was warm and soft as he spoke of his wife.

"No children, Adam?" she asked quietly.

A flicker of pain touched his eyes, then vanished. He looked at her, hesitated, and shook his head.

Allegra understood. When he had married Maggie he was still hurting from his own childhood. Bringing another child into the world had probably been the last thing he wanted. She touched the back of his hand.

"There's something I have to ask you," Adam said.

"Anything," she answered sincerely.

"I don't want to upset you, but I have to know why you sent me away."

Allegra nodded. "Of course you do. I should have told you years ago. I couldn't then, but I can now." She looked at her son, hoping he would understand her a little better after she explained.

Adam rubbed his jaw. "The passage of time somehow changes us. I've come to understand more—and learn more—as the years pass."

"I've learned too, but the road was long and

hard. At least I've been given a second chance," she said and watched him nod thoughtfully.

Allegra sat up straighter, fortifying herself for the task ahead. She sighed and patted his hand, staring past him, lost in memories of the three of them and their happiness.

Allegra and Jim had everything anyone could ever want—happiness, health, fame, and more money than they knew what to do with. The couple was blessed with a closeness that didn't happen often, especially in Hollywood.

It used to frighten her, that happiness. There seemed to be so much trouble in the world, yet none of it touched them. It was as if they were being watched over by the gods. Every movie Jim and Allegra made was a smashing hit. And Adam was such a beautiful and bright boy. She wasn't wise enough then to thank God for so much happiness. Perhaps if she had . . .

Allegra sank deeper into her reverie. Jim had been in Europe for a couple of weeks working on a movie. One morning he called and said he missed them and was going to fly home for a few days. The timing was perfect as she was in between movies. His plane was scheduled to arrive the following night at ten, but because he would never let her drive alone at night, she dropped off his Porsche at the airport in the morning. If only she had gone to pick him up. . . .

Suddenly Allegra remembered where she was. Her eyes focused on her son's face and she began speaking. "It all started the night your father died. A freak storm came in from the Pacific and the rains were horrendous. I remember pacing back and forth for what seemed like hours. And then the phone rang. It was your father. He said the plane had landed safely and he'd be home in less than an hour."

Allegra drifted off again. She'd pleaded with Jim to get a room at the airport until the rain stopped. She begged him not to drive. But he wouldn't listen. He said he couldn't wait to see them. She had a sinking feeling, a feeling of doom. She didn't know exactly what it was, but she could feel herself trembling deep inside. That's when she'd told Adam to go to bed; she sensed something terrible was about to happen.

Coming back to the present, Allegra shuddered and reached deep down inside herself. Then she continued in a soft voice. "Forty-five minutes passed. An hour. An hour and a half. I was beside myself with worry. And then the doorbell rang. I froze. Your father wouldn't ring the bell, he'd use his key. I couldn't move, Adam. The bell kept ringing and ringing and I wanted to shout to whomever it was to go away and leave me alone. But it didn't stop and finally I forced myself to get up and open the door."

Allegra's face was ashen. Adam held her in his arms and rocked her back and forth. "Two policemen were at the door," she whispered, clutching his arm. "I realized I'd been expecting them." Allegra stopped speaking and stared through Adam remembering the terror of that night. In a monotone she continued. "Your father missed a curve in the blinding rain. His car went over the edge of a cliff and he was killed instantly. When they told me he was dead I felt as if I had died too." Then she whispered, "That's when my life began to fall apart. . . ."

"You don't have to go on," Adam interrupted gently.

"But I do. I have to say it all," she said resolutely. "And hope you'll forgive me for my selfishness, although at the time I didn't know I was *being* selfish." She looked deep into his eyes. "I'm not the same person I was then."

"I know," he said almost to himself, "something happens to us in time. We love, we lose, we suffer. And through our suffering we become more tolerant and understanding of others. We find that nothing is all black or all white, but mostly gray because of the pain and hurt of events beyond our control."

Poppy

Allegra didn't seem to have heard. She was re-living in her mind the horror of that night so long ago. She had started screaming and they couldn't stop her. She kept hearing the sound of the crash. One of the policemen called a doctor and he gave her a shot and sleeping pills. She visualized the accident for years. Every time she went to sleep she would wake up screaming and the whole night would be relived over and over. . . .

"Mother?" Adam touched her arm.

Allegra blinked, her gaze focused on the pain in her son's eyes. She touched his face with a trembling hand. In a sad, quiet voice she said, "I never comforted you on the loss of your father, Adam. Instead I sent you away. You see, I thought of it as *my* loss—*my* husband gone—*my* life ruined. In my misguided selfishness you were forgotten. And then my life went downhill. I went from pills to men and back to pills. Again and again. I wanted to visit you, Adam, but I was too ashamed," she said and lowered her gaze.

"My heart aches for what I did to you. So many times I've wished that I could change things. More than anything else I wish I had kept you with me. But we can never go back—and the mistakes we make stay with us . . . until we're forgiven." Allegra looked up at her son beseechingly. "I don't feel I have the right to ask your forgiveness."

"You can ask for anything, Mother," Adam answered in a choked voice.

The old woman bowed her head. "I gave up that privilege when I sent you away," she said numbly.

"Look at me," he said and lifted her chin, holding her eyes with his. "We both need forgiveness."

Allegra took her son's face in her trembling hands. "I love you more than I could ever put into words. Of course I forgive you."

"I love you, too, Mother. And I forgive you," he whispered.

After a moment of stillness Allegra dabbed at her flushed cheeks. "How did you know where I was?" she asked.

"A few days after you called, Maggie saw an item in a gossip column about your being in the hospital. She cut it out and put it on my desk. Next to it was a quotation by Seneca. Maggie said she knew nothing about that, but I can't imagine how else it got there," he said, and Allegra smiled to herself. He reached into his jacket pocket and extracted a piece of paper from his wallet, then handed it to her.

She stared at the quotation: she knew it well.

". . . Who knows what pain is behind virtue and what fear is behind vice? No one, in short, knows what makes a man, and only God knows his thoughts, his joys, his bitternesses, his agony, the injustices committed against him and the injustices he commits . . ."

Allegra bit her lip and looked up into Adam's eyes.

"Every time I read that quotation I knew I had to come. That I had to make my peace with you," he whispered.

He understands, she thought. He truly understands.

"And that I must bring you home with me," he continued.

"Bring me *home* with you?" Allegra echoed.

Adam nodded and took her hands. "We want you to come live with us."

Allegra stared, dumbstruck.

"We both want you. And we have plenty of room so you don't have an excuse."

Still Allegra couldn't speak.

"Okay," Adam chuckled, "you can have two kittens. But no more than two."

Allegra laughed, and then her laughter dissolved into tears.

"Don't you want to come?" he asked anxiously.

She raised her eyes, tears of happiness brimming over. "Oh, Adam, of course I do. I'm . . . I'm just so overwhelmed. . . ."

He pulled her into his arms and smoothed back her snowy white hair. "We have a lot of catching up to do," he said softly and Allegra nodded in agreement.

Thank you, God, she whispered silently, closing her eyes. And you, too, child, she added.

Ten

Y ou'd better get some rest now," Adam said, easing Allegra back down onto her pillow. "I'll come back for you the day after tomorrow." He held her hands. "Maggie's going to be so happy you've agreed to stay with us. She's been wanting to meet you ever since we've been married. You're not going to believe this, but every year on Maggie's Christmas list I find a recurring wish—a wish to go with you to Grauman's Chinese Theatre so you can tell her how it felt when you stepped on the wet cement and signed your name next to your foot-print—how it feels now to be a part of a fifty-year-old Hollywood tradition. That's my Maggie. She understood you better than I did, somehow. She's an extraordinary woman. But I've already told you that, haven't I?"

Allegra's happy smile lit up her eyes. "Please tell Maggie how much I appreciate her kind offer.

I'm looking forward to meeting her, too. And tell her one of the first things we'll do is go to the Chinese Theatre."

She smiled at her son. "Adam before you go, tell me a little about yourself . . . what you do . . ."

He sat down on the bed. "At first I thought I wanted to go into music. But in college—I stayed in Europe and went to the University of Madrid—I turned to architecture. I came back to the States and apprenticed several years while working on my master's. That's where I met Maggie—she was the company secretary."

He picked up Allegra's hand. "She put up with a lot, especially in the beginning of our marriage. I was a sullen, untrusting young man then." He smiled at Allegra. "But she's worked on me all these years and there's been some improvement. In some things I'm a slow learner, though. But enough about me. We have many years ahead of us for catching up."

Allegra smiled and nodded. "I think I'll take your advice and get some sleep now. Happiness can be exhausting."

"Good night, Mother," he said, bending down to kiss her.

"Adam," Allegra said drowsily, "you're not a

figment of my imagination—are you? You really are here, aren't you?"

"Not only am I here right now, but I'm going to be here from now on," her son whispered huskily. He walked softly over to the window and pulled the drapes. Allegra smiled, sinking into a deep, restful sleep as Adam closed the door behind him.

The next morning, she woke in panic. Hadn't Adam closed the drapes last night? Then why was her room filled with bright sunlight? She looked around frantically for some reassurance that he had really been there.

"Good morning," Poppy said from the doorway.

Allegra's head turned quickly toward the cheery voice. "Did you . . . ?" she asked, indicating the drapes.

"Who else?" Poppy answered with twinkling eyes.

Allegra sighed deeply with relief. "For a minute I thought . . ."

"It was no dream. Adam was here," the little girl said firmly and walked over to the bed.

"Thank God," the old woman sighed, falling back against the pillows.

"Let's go for a walk in the garden this morning," Poppy suggested, a tinge of sadness in her voice.

Allegra nodded. "I'm leaving tomorrow morning. Adam's coming for me. I'm going to live with him and Maggie," she said softly, watching the child's face closely.

"I know."

Of course you know, Allegra thought. "But I'm going to keep visiting the hospital and bringing books and things to people. I'm not going to just sit around and do nothing for the rest of my life," she said.

Poppy smiled fondly. "Allegra Alexander sit around and do nothing! Never! You have too much to give, too much to offer."

Allegra returned her smile. "Hand me my robe, child, and we'll go out to your garden."

They walked along slowly and silently, isolated from the rest of the world. At the fountain where Poppy had taken Allegra in the wheelchair the day that now seemed eons away, they sat down on the wooden bench. The little girl reached for Allegra's hand. "You see how God works, Allegra? In His own time. Not always as quickly as we'd like, but when He feels the time is right for everyone involved."

"I've had so many miracles lately . . ."

"You helped to make them. God always works *through* us. By opening yourself to love and forgiveness you allowed Him to act."

"Look at all the time I wasted, child," she said.

Poppy looked into Allegra's eyes. "We can only do what we're capable of doing at the moment. You weren't ready before."

"Perhaps you're right," Allegra said and watched the precious child smile at her lovingly.

"You're very happy, aren't you?" the little girl asked.

"Oh, I can't begin to tell you how happy I am. It's like a lifetime of waiting is finally over."

"It is."

Allegra squeezed the small hand. "I only wish that somehow you could . . ."

"Let's pray," Poppy interrupted gently. "Let's thank God for giving you such happiness."

Allegra felt tears prick her eyelids. She's slipping away, she thought. She's going to go out of my life just the way she came in. And I'm not going to be able to do anything about it. When she looked over at Poppy, the little girl's small face was raised to the heavens.

"I don't know who you are, child, but thank you for coming into my life," she whispered.

Poppy

Poppy lowered her face. "Let's pick some flowers for your room," she suggested, getting up.

"Won't we get in trouble?"

"Oh, phooey. Flowers were meant to be enjoyed. There are so many, they'll never miss a few. You would like some, wouldn't you?" she asked.

"I'd love some."

"I know just the ones. Come on."

Poppy led the way deep into her garden and stooped down in front of a sea of flowers, the sun turning her hair to fire. Taking a small pair of scissors from her pocket, she began cutting, her hands working busily among the stems. Standing up, she handed a bouquet to Allegra, and her warm hand lingered on the old woman's.

"Why, they're poppies," Allegra cried in pleasure. "And look at this one! It's red-gold. The same color as your hair."

"Do you like them?" Poppy asked.

"I love them. I'm going to keep this one," she said, indicating the red-gold flower, "and press it in a book. Then whenever I want to feel you near me, I'll get it out and look at it." She touched the girl's soft cheek.

Poppy's eyes sparkled with unshed tears. "I will be with you always, Allegra. Always." The little girl suddenly threw her arms around the old woman's waist and hugged her. Allegra held her close, the velvety flowers nodding against the child's tousled hair.

They walked back toward the hospital in silence, the old woman clutching her bouquet of poppies, occasionally stroking the one that reminded her of her small friend.

"I have some books to give away and there are a few people I want to give my new address to. Will you come back later and visit with me?" Allegra asked, suddenly afraid she might not see the child again.

Poppy nodded. "I'll stop by tonight and help you get your things together."

"I'd like that." She stood and watched the little girl walk away until she was out of sight. Then Allegra turned and went into the hospital.

After dinner she pulled out her small suitcase and opened it on the bed. How would she ever fit all the books she'd accumulated into it? Betty had been a dear and made several runs to the bookstore for her. Maybe she should leave most of them for the patients. She could always buy new ones. She was still pondering which ones to take when Poppy came in.

"I brought you a going-away present." She handed Allegra a small package.

Allegra quickly unwrapped the box and opened it. Inside lay a delicate gold locket on a long, slender chain. "Oh, thank you, child. It's lovely. It's one of the nicest presents I've ever received." Opening the catch of the locket, she looked up. "But there are no pictures in it."

"I left that for you to do."

"But . . ."

"Let me help you with the packing," Poppy said and walked over to the bed. "Which books are you going to take?"

"Those over there, I guess," she answered and clasped the chain around her neck.

After they finished, Allegra was reluctant to let Poppy leave. "Stay with me awhile, child." Poppy nodded, her hand in Allegra's. Allegra's eyes grew heavy, and she murmured, "I'll see you in the morning, won't I?" Poppy's sad little smile, half hidden by her unruly red hair, was the last thing Allegra remembered before falling asleep, their fingers firmly laced together.

The sun woke her and she glanced quickly at the clock. I'll have to hurry. Adam will be here in an hour. And where is Poppy? How can I leave without seeing her? First things first, she told herself and hurriedly put her clothes on.

The locket was still around her neck, and she

tucked it inside her dress—close to her heart—and touched it gently through the thin material.

Even though she knew it was futile, Allegra was compelled to make the attempt to find Poppy. She walked to the nurses' station. "Where's the children's ward?" she asked.

"Sixth floor."

The elevator halted with a jerk, and Allegra stepped off and looked around. She stopped a young nurse walking by. "Excuse me, do you have a red-haired patient on this floor? A little girl about nine?"

"What's her name?"

Allegra paused. "I only know her first name—Poppy."

"That's probably a nickname. Sorry, I don't remember any redheads lately."

"You'd remember this one if you'd ever met her," Allegra said, walking to the elevator.

Back again on the first floor, Allegra looked around for someone she could ask about Poppy. Betty was wheeling a tray in her direction.

"Hi, Allegra." Betty greeted her with a smile. "All ready to go home?"

"Just about. Have you seen a young red-haired girl around this morning?"

Betty shook her head. "A relative of yours?"

"No. A friend. Thanks, anyway," Allegra said and walked away.

Her eyes searched the hall and lit up when she thought she saw Poppy entering the chapel. Allegra made her way to the small room and opened the door. Except for one large candle, the room was in darkness. Standing in the back, she waited for her eyes to adjust to the dim light. When she was finally able to see she looked around, but Poppy wasn't there.

Allegra sank down in one of the pews, utterly defeated. She closed her eyes. Another loss to bear, she thought and touched the locket with trembling fingers.

Then, as clearly as if the child were sitting next to her, the old woman heard Poppy say, "I will be with you always, Allegra."

Allegra nodded and bowed her head in prayer. A few minutes later she raised her eyes to the altar and smiled radiantly. For, in the silence, she had divined that Poppy was a gift from God, and once given would never be taken away.

Eleven

When Allegra returned to her room, Adam was waiting. They embraced as naturally as if there had never been a time when they hadn't. Then Adam asked, "Ready?"

Allegra nodded. She walked over to the window, hoping to see Poppy looking up at her. But deep in her heart, Allegra knew Poppy wouldn't be there.

Adam picked up her suitcase. "Come, Mother, Maggie's waiting outside," he said gently. Then he grinned mischievously. "I'm parked in a tow-away zone."

She smiled and moved toward the door. "Oh wait . . . my flowers," she said, taking the delicate red and orange poppies out of the vase and wrapping the long stems in tissues.

Maggie was leaning against the car. She hurried toward them. Her strawberry blond hair shone in the sunlight and she smiled brightly at Allegra, holding out her hands. Allegra knew instantly that she would grow to love this woman who had so willingly opened her heart and her home to her.

Inside the car, Maggie began telling Allegra about the house. "We have a guest room at one end that hasn't been used very much. It'll be perfect for you. It has its own bath and a small study. And the sliding glass door opens out to a little garden that you can have for your own, if you'd like."

"It sounds wonderful! I'd love having my own garden." Allegra caressed the flowers.

Maggie's gaze went to the bouquet. "They're beautiful," she said softly and reached back to touch the red-gold poppy.

Adam cleared his throat and turned around for a moment.

"There's also something else."

"What is it?" Allegra asked.

"Well, we didn't want you to be lonely for even a minute, so we went out to get you a kitten. But we couldn't decide between the white one and the black one, so we got both. We can pick them up tomorrow."

"Adam . . . Maggie." Allegra moved her head from side to side. "I don't know what to say. So much is happening so suddenly," and she touched the red-gold poppy again.

"We're just happy to have you with us. To be a family," Maggie said, reaching back to take the old woman's hand.

"Thank you. You don't know how much I've wanted that."

Maggie smiled a sad smile. "Yes I do," she whispered, squeezing Allegra's hand softly.

When Adam pulled the car to a stop, Allegra looked out at a beautiful white Spanish-style house. Lovely trees dotted the lawn, but it was the profusion of flowers that caught her attention. They were everywhere, some snuggling close to the house, others lining the path to the front door. There were so many, she couldn't begin to distinguish the varieties.

Adam came around and opened the doors for Allegra and Maggie, then stood with his arms around both of them. What a loving, peaceful home, Allegra thought. I am surely blessed to be part of it. Still clutching the poppies, she smiled up at Adam and then at Maggie.

147

"Come on," Maggie said, taking her arm. "Let's go to your rooms. You can put the flowers in a vase. Adam will bring your suitcase."

If only Poppy were here, Allegra thought, touching the locket through her dress.

Adam dropped the suitcase on the Mexican tile floor and Maggie helped her unpack. "Why, you have more books here than clothes! I can see we need to go on a shopping spree," Maggie said, hands on her slender hips.

Allegra laughed. "I had more use for books in the hospital than I did for clothes."

"Maybe so, but you're not in the hospital anymore." Maggie hugged Allegra. "Would you like to see the rest of the house or do you want to rest before lunch?"

"I'd like to see the house," Allegra said and followed Maggie and Adam down the hall.

Allegra loved every room. She felt as if she had come home. The sunny yellow and white kitchen with dotted swiss curtains and the cozy breakfast room were bright and cheerful. Adam's library was filled with hundreds of books, and she couldn't wait to look through them.

"This is the living room," Adam said, leading Allegra down white carpeted steps into a large spacious room.

Suddenly Allegra gasped. A band tightened around her heart. Lightheaded, she fought to steady herself. Adam and Maggie looked shocked by her ashen face. "I'll get some water," Maggie said and rushed out of the room.

"Mother, are you all right? Here, sit down." Adam led her to a huge, overstuffed sofa. "You look like you've seen a ghost. Maybe we're overdoing it for one day."

Allegra squeezed Adam's hand. "I'm okay. I just felt a little faint for a minute. It's passed now." She breathed deeply, and when Maggie returned and handed her the glass of water she sipped it slowly.

Setting the glass down on the coffee table, Allegra mustered enough courage to look again at the portrait over the fireplace. The portrait of a young girl with copper hair tumbling over her brow, wearing a blue dress and a delicate gold locket. The locket that now lay next to Allegra's heart.

She bit her bottom lip to stop its trembling. Making her voice as casual as she could, Allegra asked, "Whose portrait is that?"

Adam's voice was low and sad. "That's our daughter." He reached for Maggie's hand.

"But I . . . I thought . . ." Allegra's heart hammered furiously.

"She's dead, Mother. I didn't want to upset you when you asked in the hospital." He ran his fingers through his hair. "We lost her ten years ago."

Allegra stared at the portrait, barely breathing. "How old was she when . . . ?"

"She was nine."

The room spun around crazily and Allegra shook her head to steady herself. She had to ask one more question. "Adam," she said, her hand on his arm, "what was my granddaughter's name?"

Several seconds went by as he stared at the painting. Maggie squeezed his hand and turned to Allegra, putting her arm around the old woman. "Because of her red hair," she said softly, "we called her Poppy."

Of course, Allegra thought. Leaning on Adam, she rose from the deep couch. At the top of the steps she placed her hand over her heart and felt for the locket beneath her dress before turning around to seek once more the wise gray eyes in the portrait. In the stillness of the room she clearly heard

Poppy's voice, "I will be with you always, Allegra. Always."

The old woman brushed away a tear and smiled. I don't doubt that for a minute, child. Not for a minute.

—In memory of my daughter, Poppy—

About the Author

A native of New Jersey, Barbara Larriva now lives in Scottsdale, Arizona, with her son Greg, their black cat Shalom, and their ferret Flash. *Poppy*, the author's first novel, is the result of her firm belief in faith, persistence, and prayer.